HORSE TALES

Horse Tales

COLLECTED BY JUNE CREBBIN

ILLUSTRATED BY

INGA MOORE

WALKER BOOKS
AND SUBSIDIARIES
LONDON • BOSTON • SYDNEY • AUCKLAND

CONTENTS

Difficult Horses

Dream Horses

From the Horse's Mouth

Horses in Danger

Horses to the Rescue

Difficult Horses

If at all possible, I avoid difficult horses! Just as Kate tries to avoid riding Tania, "The Orange Pony".

I prefer my mounts to be well mannered and obedient; whether in a dressage test or out on a hack in the beautiful Leicestershire countryside where I live.

Oscar is such a mount. Yet even he has his difficult moments. Once I spent a very long time encouraging him to go past a road sign which had fallen over and was lying on the grass verge!

Dusty has a real battle on her hands with "The Snow Pony". But, like Alexander with Bucephalus, she knows that horses are often difficult because they are frightened.

Take away the fear. Then – who knows?

The Orange Pony
Wendy Douthwaite

In this extract, part of the first chapter, Kate arrives at Oakhouse Stables and is faced with the ride she has been dreading.

"OH, NO! Not the Orange Pony!"

Kate felt the colour drain from her face as she spoke. Janet Delwood, the owner of Oakhouse Stables, looked at her in surprise.

"But, Kate," she said, reproachfully, "Tania's a lovely ride. I know she's a bit ... well ... *difficult* with other ponies, but I'm sure you'll manage." She smiled encouragingly at the eleven-year-old, who looked back at her with such wide-eyed horror. "You don't get much riding practice on old Darkie, you know," she continued. "We really keep him for our beginners – he's so slow and reliable. But you've been coming to Oakhouse Stables for four months now – it's time you moved on to a more *lively* mount."

"But I *like* riding Darkie."

"Well, I can't help it, Kate. Darkie's got a nasty cough and I don't want to send him out until the vet has seen him. You wouldn't want to risk making him ill, would you?"

"Of course not," Kate replied, hastily. She sensed a slight impatience in Janet's voice, and she was aware of Paula Holt watching her from outside Lancelot's stable, her eyes scornful.

"It's all right," Kate added quickly. "I'll ride her."

Janet looked relieved. "I'm sure you'll enjoy it," she said, turning back towards the tack room to answer the shrill call of the stable telephone.

Kate's spirits were low as she pushed her bicycle across the stable yard and propped it against the back wall of the tack room. Out of sight of the others, she fought back the tears which threatened. How could she explain to Janet – or to anyone – the fear that overtook her when she thought of riding the Orange Pony.

In fact, Kate thought miserably as she delved into her saddlebag in search of an apple for Darkie, how could she explain to anyone – or even to herself – how terrified she felt of riding *any* pony, except perhaps Darkie. She loved *ponies*, but riding them frightened her. Darkie was different, she thought fondly. Little Darkie was quite old. Janet was not sure, but she thought he was about twenty-two. Added to that, he had a very gentle disposition; and even Kate, who was his greatest fan, was bound to admit that he *was* a trifle lazy. To encourage Darkie to break into a trot was a tiring experience for his rider's legs, and to make him canter was practically unthinkable!

As Kate approached the stable block, the subject of her thoughts put his head over the end door. Two small black ears were pricked expectantly between a wild, unruly mop of mane, and a pair of gentle brown eyes watched Kate's approach with interest. Below his soft black muzzle, Darkie's lower lip hung, trembling with anticipation.

No one could feel afraid of riding such a dear old thing; but the Orange Pony ... Kate shuddered at the thought, as she rubbed Darkie between his ears before sliding back the bolt of the stable door. The apple was soon gone as Darkie munched happily, pushing his soft nose into Kate's hand in search of more.

"Don't worry," said Kate, "I've more for later on." She smoothed his neck and tickled his nose. "You're a greedy little pony, you know," she told him fondly. "Still, I mustn't tell you off," she continued. "You're not very well today, are you?"

As if he understood, Darkie put his head down and coughed.

"Oh, poor little Darkie," Kate murmured. "I hope you'll be all right."

The light from the doorway darkened, as Paula looked over the stable door.

"Time to get going," she called, and Kate was sure that there was a malicious gleam in her eye.

Kate let herself out of Darkie's stable, her stomach

turning over and over in anticipation. Looking towards the group of ponies gathered at the far end of the stable yard, she wondered if she should simply go over to Janet and tell her that she could not go. Then she saw the watchful eyes of Paula, who stood beside Lancelot, the big powerful grey which Paula liked to ride. Holding on to Lancelot's reins, she was in charge of Tania's reins, too, but she held the other pony at arm's length. The red ribbon was tied firmly in place at the top of Tania's tail, warning other riders that she might kick.

As she walked reluctantly towards the ponies, Kate found herself wondering why they all called Tania the Orange Pony. She was, in fact, a pale dun colour, with black mane and tail, black stockings and black-tipped ears – which now were flat against her head. Kate's stomach began to churn again as she saw Tania's expression; mean was the only way in which she could describe it.

"Could you take her away from the others?" Paula said. "She makes them nervous." Kate was surprised to see that Paula, too, looked uncertain.

Plucking up her courage, Kate took hold of Tania's reins and tried to lead her away. Tania flattened her ears even more and looked at Kate sullenly.

"Come on, oh *please*, Tania, come on," Kate begged, tugging at the reins.

Janet came to her rescue. "Hold both reins firmly, close to her chin, Kate," she said. "That's it. Now, don't try to pull her; go round to the other side and push her head away from you and give her shoulder a little push." When Kate did as Janet suggested, Tania turned, and Kate was able to move her away from the other ponies.

"It's no good trying to compete in a tugging match with a pony," Janet advised, holding Tania's reins while Kate mounted. "The pony will always win because it's stronger. Now – how does she feel?"

"Not too bad," said Kate, doubtfully.

"Well, try and keep her away from the others." Janet looked at Tania thoughtfully. "It's a shame that she's the way she is with other ponies," she said. "I didn't realize when I bought her last September. She's so pretty in the summer – a lovely apricot, almost orange colour. She's very frightened of the other ponies, though, and that's why she kicks and bites."

"*Frightened* of them?" Kate echoed, looking surprised.

"Well, you know what they say," Janet laughed as she moved away to mount Charlie, her big dark bay cob, "attack is the best form of defence!"

Kate held Tania back while the rest of the ride moved off, and then squeezed her tentatively with her heels. Her heart was pounding as Tania moved away and began to walk behind the other ponies. Kate had seen Tania in action during other rides, when her rider had allowed her to come too close to another pony. Back would go Tania's ears and out would go her neck. Bared teeth would nip the hindquarters of the other pony, which would squeal with pain and annoyance. Sometimes Tania's hindquarters would swing round as she aimed a kick at the unfortunate other pony. Then a ripple of disturbance would run through the group of ponies, and someone would shout, "Watch out – it's the Orange Pony again!"

And I'm riding her, Kate thought despairingly. I shan't be able to manage, I know I shan't. Her hands trembled. I'll make a fool of myself and Paula will give that horrible snigger. Kate saw Tania's ear flick back. She *knows* I'm frightened, Kate thought. That'll make her even worse.

Kate tried to quieten her trembling hands, and gingerly eased herself more comfortably into the saddle. She had to admit that the Orange Pony *did* have a nice swinging stride; it was very different from little Darkie's slow plod. But at least she was safe on Darkie. On the Orange Pony, she didn't know *what* might happen.

Up at the front, Janet raised her riding crop as a signal to trot. "Trot on!" she called, squeezing Charlie into a gentle trot. The other ponies followed, and Kate squeezed Tania into a trot, too. They were well behind the others, and Tania trotted out briskly, her ears pricked forward for once. It was a bouncy trot, but comfortable, and Kate was surprised to find she was almost enjoying herself. Soon, however, they caught up with the ambling pony at the back, and Tania slowed down, putting her ears back. Kate felt her stiffen.

"Steady, girl," she said, trying to sound reassuring, but her voice quavered.

Janet called a halt at the main road, and then they all

crossed over. This was the part that Kate had dreaded. The ponies' hooves were thudding gently now, for they had turned off the road on to the Downs. They trotted sedately down the wide grassy path, and then Janet halted. All the ponies stopped, and Kate held Tania back.

"We'll have a little canter now, shall we?" Janet said. Kate's hands tightened on the reins. She might be all right if she could only keep Tania away from everyone else.

Janet turned Charlie round and pointed back the way they had come. "We'll canter back along the ride, and then we'll do some practice drill in the open," she said.

Trembling with fright, Kate turned Tania round and tried to keep her well away, but the pony sensed the approach of the others; her ears flattened against her head and her hindquarters stiffened.

"Come on, everyone!" It was Paula who shouted and kicked her pony into action. Pushing past, too close to Tania, she set off at a fast canter, shrieking at her pony, "Go on, Lancelot – go on!"

The other ponies surged past Tania, and the dun pony kicked out wildly. Kate lost one stirrup and, as she did so, Tania set off after the others.

Kate had never been so fast on a pony before. Terrified, she clung to the pommel of the saddle and fumbled with her foot until, at last, she found the lost stirrup. She moved her grip from the saddle to Tania's black mane, and then she gathered up the dropped reins. The ground sped past at an alarming rate.

"I'll never, *never* ride again," thought Kate, as she and Tania galloped on. They were catching up with the other ponies. Finding a gap, Tania galloped through, her ears flat against her head and her long black tail streaming out behind her. For a moment, Kate saw the amazed faces of the other riders, and then she and Tania were on their own, galloping down the long grassy ride.

Some of Kate's fear had left her, and she started to pull on the reins. Tania's pace began to ease. Kate pulled again, and at last they were cantering. Tania's ears were forward now, and Kate was amazed to find herself enjoying this ride; the smooth, steady stride of the dun pony; the gentle thudding of hooves; Tania's black mane brushing against her face.

The Snow Pony
Alison Lester

*Dusty is eleven when she first sees the Snow Pony,
a beautiful silver grey brumby mare. The following year,
her father, Jack — an Australian cattle farmer —
catches the pony and brings it home. But he warns Dusty
that the mare may be too wild to ride.*

DUSTY sat on the top rail of the stockyards' fence, gripping so hard her knuckles were white. She stayed very still so as not to frighten the Snow Pony. Jack was about to ride her for the first time. He'd mouthed the mare and saddled her and driven her in long reins, and now the moment of truth had come when they would see how she'd react to having a rider on her back. Last night, when they'd talked about it, Jack hadn't been optimistic.

"She's done everything I've asked her to, I have to admit. But the minute she doesn't understand something she panics, and it's a blind panic, as though she just switches off."

"Why don't you let me ride her first?" Dusty asked. "She never panics with me."

Jack shook his head and Rita nodded in agreement. "No way," they said together and Dusty knew they meant it.

The Snow Pony stayed still as Jack put his foot into the stirrup. She'd grown taller since that night they first saw her in the moonlight, a year ago, and stood at about fifteen hands, so she wasn't really a pony any more, but her name had stuck. Her new spring coat gleamed like gunmetal and the scatter of dots on her rump looked more like a trick of light than white dapples. The scar on her shoulder stood out in a dark, ragged Z. She was still slight, so the bridle, headstall, stock saddle, breastplate and crupper seemed too big for her, as though there was hardly any horse beneath all that gear. That was until Jack gently settled his weight onto her back. Then, before Dusty's very eyes, she grew – getting bigger, swelling – until she exploded into a series of leaps and bounds and bucks that jolted Jack around like a rag doll. He stuck like glue, trying to pull her head up and spurring her forward every time she bucked. Finally she was exhausted, "bucked out", and she propped, legs splayed and sides heaving, dripping with sweat. Jack sat on her for a little while, panting himself, then pushed her forward and she walked quietly around the yard.

"That's more like it." He rewarded her with a pat on the neck. "Good girl." But even as he was saying it, he was looking at Dusty and shaking his head.

Dusty felt like howling, but she blinked the tears back. It was shocking to see her horse resisting so violently, and she knew she'd never stay on a bronco like that, but she knew in her heart that the Snow Pony wouldn't buck like that with her. Dad thought he knew everything about horses, but he didn't know about this one, she thought bitterly. He was just going to muck her up.

When Dusty got home from school the next day, Jack had ridden the Snow Pony again and had the bruises to prove it.

"She got rid of me all right," Jack said as he limped about the kitchen. "It's a long time since I've been bucked off a horse, but she did it. She pelted me off. I got back on and stayed on, so I reckon I won the fight, but she certainly won that round."

Rita was chopping up vegetables at the sink and Dusty saw her mouth squash up like a chook's bum, the way it always did when she had something difficult to say.

"What is it, Mum?" She waited for it.

Rita kept chopping. She knew how much the horse meant to Dusty.

"I don't think she's going to work out. I know you love her, but I don't think the Snow Pony is ever going to be a suitable horse for you." She looked at Jack for support and he nodded, rubbing his grazed elbow at the same time.

24

"I don't know anyone who has a better way with horses than your father. Horses *like* him, they go well for him. The fact that the mare is resisting him so determinedly probably means that she just can't be ridden. She might just be too wild."

Dusty walked down the passage to her room and flopped on the bed. Sue *knew* the Snow Pony was a good horse, her parents just couldn't see it. Stewie crept in, looking mysterious, hands tucked up under his pyjama top.

"I got you a happy tablet, Dusty." He smiled and held out a Tim Tam for her. "They eat these in outer space you know. Really." Dusty looked doubtful so he kept going. "It's true. Whenever they get earth-sick, they have a Tim Tam. Cheers 'em up just like that."

"You're an idiot, Stewie." Dusty pulled his hair into spikes with her chocolaty fingers. "But thanks."

"You're not wild, are you?" Dusty rubbed the Snow Pony around her eyes, brushing the dried sweat from her face. The corners of her mouth were raw where she had fought against the bit, and her coat was stiff and shiny where Jack had hosed her down. "You dumb horse. You've learnt all your other lessons: tying up, getting washed, going on the truck, getting saddled."

The Snow Pony nestled her head into the front of Dusty's shirt, and it felt as though she was trying to hide there. Dusty thought back to the time she'd first seen her up at The Plains, wild and beautiful, happy with her pinto pal, and wished that she hadn't begged Jack to catch her. If the mare didn't turn out, what would happen to her? Would they just turn her loose again? She might never find her mate. She might not be able to survive in the wild any more.

"I'm sorry, girl," Dusty whispered in the fluffy grey ear. "It's my fault all this has happened to you, but let him ride you. It's just one more thing to learn. I know you can do it."

As Dusty climbed out of the yards she glanced back at the Snow Pony. The mare looked so sad and woebegone, standing like a waif in the dusty yards, that it brought tears to her eyes. She was still teary when she stepped into the bright fluorescent light of the kitchen and her father pulled her on to his knee.

"Don't be sad, mate. I'll give her a week. I'll ride her every day for a week, and if she hasn't come good by then we'll have to give her a miss. Okay? Do you think that's fair enough?"

Dusty nodded her head sadly. It was fair, but it wasn't hopeful. She didn't think the Snow Pony would ever let Jack ride her.

The Snow Pony stood in the furthest corner of the yards with her rump turned towards the house. Her hay lay uneaten on the ground, even though she looked pinched and hungry. She didn't turn as Dusty walked across the yard, calling her softly, but when the girl's arms circled her neck she sighed and dropped her head. The week was up. Today, when Jack had ridden her, she had bucked as furiously as she had on the first day.

"Poor girl." Dusty rubbed her behind the ear. "You can't help it, can you?" As she stood there in the warm spring evening, Dusty knew she was going to do the thing she had wanted to do ever since her father had started breaking in the Snow Pony.

She fetched the tack box from the shed and brushed the dust and dried sweat from the mare's coat, combed her mane and tail and picked out her hooves. She took the crupper off the saddle; she knew the Snow Pony hated it. Then she saddled her, carefully smoothing all the creases out of the saddle blanket and lifting the saddle up slowly on to her back, with the girth, breastplate and stirrups folded over the top so nothing would flap or frighten her. She measured the stirrup leathers against her arm and shortened them to her length, then buckled up the chin strap of her riding helmet and peered through the rails of the yards towards the house. Good, no one was outside. Her parents would kill her if they knew what she was doing. A voice in her head was saying they were right, it was a stupid idea, a childish fantasy that she could ride a horse that had defeated her father. But another voice, a louder voice, said she *could* do it, that the Snow Pony trusted her, would do anything for her.

Dusty gathered the reins and a big clump of mane on the Snow Pony's withers, and moved in very close to her

shoulder. "Steady, girl." She put her foot in the stirrup, keeping her back facing the Snow Pony's head, and gently swung up into the saddle, trying to copy her father's calm, economical movement.

The mare didn't react as Dusty settled into the saddle and felt frantically for her off-side stirrup. Usually her boot slid straight in, but this was Jack's saddle, and the iron was in a slightly different spot. "Hang on, girl." She was shaking like a leaf. So much for staying calm so that the Snow Pony wouldn't get upset, she thought.

"Gotcha!" Her foot finally found the stirrup. She took a huge breath, then let it out again, then just sat there, breathing in and blowing out until she stopped shaking.

The Snow Pony slowly turned her head and looked quizzically at her boot as if to say, "Are you right? Are you ready now?" Dusty laughed out loud and suddenly it felt as if everything was going to be all right. She clicked her tongue and squeezed the Snow Pony with her legs, and the mare moved forward. She felt different from any other horse Dusty had ever ridden: narrow, wobbly and unsure, as though she didn't know where to go. Horses that were used to being ridden moved off with a purpose – they knew they were going somewhere – but this mare was like a ship without a rudder. Dusty guided her more deliberately with her legs and reins, and it felt as if she was exaggerating everything, but the Snow Pony seemed to like it. It didn't feel as though she was going to buck.

Dusty rode her around the yard three times, then

turned and went the other way. She stopped and backed her up, then went forward again. The Snow Pony did everything she asked. Finally, Dusty plucked up courage and pushed her into a trot. They did circles and figure-eights in the yard, and all the while the Snow Pony had one ear back listening to Dusty's voice. "Good girl, good girl." They were going so beautifully that Dusty thought they might as well canter. So she sat down in the saddle, clicked her tongue and the Snow Pony broke into a canter. It felt as though she was floating, flying through the dust-filled air like an angel. She brought her back to a trot, turned and cantered that way too, then trotted down to a halt.

Dusty felt so happy it seemed as though her heart was going to jump out of her chest. "Oh, you good thing, you good girl!" She reached down and patted the Snow Pony on her sweating neck. When she looked up she could see the lights of the house glowing yellow in the evening light. "Come on, girl," she said to her horse. "Let's go and show them."

Bucephalus: A King's Horse
Alice Gall & Fleming Crew

*This story from Ancient Greece tells how
Bucephalus, a fiery stallion, becomes the trusted warhorse
of Alexander the Great.*

"SAY no more, Orestes. My mind is made up. The horse Bucephalus shall be sold."

It was on a summer day, more than two thousand years ago, that these words were spoken by Philonicus, a wealthy man of Thessaly in Greece. The two men, Philonicus the master and Orestes his slave, stood under a plane tree at one end of a green field in which a number of horses were pasturing. Around this field stretched on all sides the wide flat plains of Thessaly. And far to the north rose the lofty peaks of Mount Olympus, believed in those days to be the home of mighty gods who ruled the world.

Both master and slave were dressed in the long flowing robes of their time. But the master's robe was richly embroidered in silver, as were the sandals on his feet. About his thick brown hair he wore a band of purple. Philonicus was a man accustomed to being obeyed, and when he had spoken these words to Orestes he turned away.

But the slave put out a hand as though to detain him. "Master," he said earnestly, "there is not in all Greece another horse like Bucephalus."

"Well do I know that, Orestes," Philonicus answered, "and his new master shall pay a princely sum for him. I mean to sell him to King Philip of Macedon."

"King Philip of Macedon!" the slave repeated in amazement.

"None other," replied Philonicus. "King Philip knows horses. His army rides into battle mounted on splendid chargers fit for the war-god Mars himself. And it is said that Philip of Macedon would rather lose six generals than one good horse of war. He will find use for Bucephalus."

"Master," Orestes pleaded, "you would not send Bucephalus into the cruel wars of Macedon? You know well how gentle has been his training. Never has he felt the sting of the lash. Surely, my master, you will not sell Bucephalus to King Philip."

"Such is my plan," Philonicus answered shortly, and a look of greed came into his eyes as he added, "King Philip's wars have brought him much wealth. His treasury is full. I mean to make him pay handsomely for Bucephalus." And with this Philonicus walked away.

After his master had gone, Orestes stood looking sadly off towards Olympus. If only some god would help him save Bucephalus, he thought. But the great mountain seemed very far away and he, Orestes, was a slave. He could expect little help from the gods.

Presently he whistled softly, a long clear note, and in a moment or two Bucephalus appeared at the edge of a grove of oak trees far across the field. Trotting over to where Orestes stood, the beautiful dark bay horse lowered his head so that the slave might stroke his nose and pull his silky ears. For a while he stood so, scarcely moving at all, and then suddenly he thrust his muzzle forward, gave Orestes a playful shove, and was off down the field like the wind, his head held high, his tail streaming straight out behind him.

This was a favourite trick of his and Orestes always expected it. But today the slave could not laugh; his heart was too heavy. From the time Bucephalus was a tiny colt Orestes had looked after him, feeding him and caring for him each day. It was Orestes who had put a bridle on him for the first time and taught him to carry a man on his back.

Bucephalus had not liked this. The bit hurt his tender mouth and having a man on his back seemed a strange thing. But Orestes had been so kind and patient that soon the strangeness wore off, and Bucephalus no longer rebelled but gladly carried the slave, mile after mile, across the broad flat plains.

Thessaly is a fair land, and for Bucephalus life was pleasant. There was the wide green pasture with its soft grass and its grove of oak trees where the shade was welcome on hot afternoons. And there was a stream of cool water where he drank when he was thirsty and in whose quiet pools he stood, knee deep, when the flies and insects annoyed him.

What would the life of Bucephalus be after this, Orestes wondered, as he watched the young horse galloping over the field? King Philip of Macedon was a powerful king, he knew, for the tales of his wars and conquests had spread over all that part of the world. It was said that even now he was planning greater wars, that he longed to rule over a mighty empire, and dreamt of a day when all Greece should be his.

And now because Philonicus was greedy for gold and King Philip of Macedon was greedy for power, Bucephalus was to have a new master!

On a morning late that summer King Philip of Macedon and his son Alexander, a lad of sixteen years, were walking through the palace gardens. They were on their way to the parade grounds to inspect the soldiers at their morning drill. But they had gone only a little way when they were met by a guardsman who saluted and stood to attention.

"Have you a message?" King Philip asked.

"Yes, Sire," the guardsman answered. "A stranger from Thessaly would see you."

"What is his errand?"

"Sire, he would sell you a horse," the guardsman told him.

"A horse!" King Philip thundered. "And you come to me with such a thing. Do you take me for a stable boy? This is an affair for some petty groom. If the horse is sound, let him be bought."

"The horse is a good one, Sire," the guardsman replied, "but the price is very high and the officers who are charged with such matters feared your displeasure."

"We have gold to purchase what we need," the king told him sharply. "Go, tell my men to use their wits."

"The price the stranger asks is thirteen talents, Sire."

King Philip looked at the guardsman in amazement. "Thirteen talents!" he exclaimed. "Why, such a price would scarce be paid for twenty horses! Dismiss the man at once. Tell him King Philip is no fool."

The guardsman saluted again and turned to go, but the boy Alexander called to him. "Wait, Simonides," he said. "The stranger comes from Thessaly, did you say?"

"From Thessaly," replied the guardsman.

"It is a land of splendid horses," Alexander said. "Let us have a look at him, father. Who knows? He may excel all horses in your stables even as you excel all other men in Macedon."

King Philip looked down at his son and laughed. "Yours is a sound head, my son," he said, laying his hand on the boy's shoulder. "Your words are well spoken. We shall see this stranger and his horse."

"Have this man of Thessaly bring his horse to the west riding field," the king told the guardsman. "And have trainers from my stables there, to put the animal through its paces."

When King Philip and young Alexander reached the riding field they found a number of the king's trainers already awaiting them.

"Where is this stranger from Thessaly and his horse?" the king asked impatiently.

"The Thessalonian comes yonder, Sire," said one of the men pointing towards the stables, "but the horse is being fed a measure of oats by the Thessalonian's slave."

King Philip laughed aloud. "What say you to that, Alexander?" he exclaimed. "A king must stand waiting while a slave feeds a horse!"

The boy Alexander made no answer, for just then the Thessalonian, accompanied by a guardsman, came and knelt before the king.

"Rise, man of Thessaly," King Philip bade him. "Your land of Greece, beyond Olympus, is not unknown to me. I have seen its beautiful cities, its splendid temples, and its wide, fertile plains. A fine land it is. But tell me," he broke off, "what of this horse who now eats his measure of oats in my stables? I would know about him, for if he be worth but half the price you ask he must still be a wondrous horse."

"You shall see for yourself, oh King," Philonicus replied. "He is a mount the gods might envy you. I am asking thirteen talents for him, but were he yours you would not part with him for many times that sum."

"Do you hear that, Alexander?" the king asked, turning towards his son. "What think you of the Thessalonian's words?"

"Why think of them at all, father?" the boy replied. "The horse himself will speak a truer tale than many words. See! Here he comes!"

From the stables across the riding field came the horse with the slave Orestes on his back. Alexander grasped his father's arm excitedly and the two of them stood looking in admiration. "He is indeed a splendid horse," exclaimed the king at last.

Bucephalus was quivering with nervousness. These were strange surroundings to him. Strange voices were all about him and he had eaten his oats in a strange stable, with men he did not know staring at him. He would have been badly frightened now if Orestes had not spoken to him encouragingly and patted his neck.

"Look, father," said Alexander. "Do you note the fine slender legs, the long body, and the narrow, well-shaped head?"

"Ay," his father answered, and then turning to Philonicus he said: "You shall have your thirteen talents, unless my trainers find some hidden flaw in him."

Two of the trainers stepped forward and grasped the bridle, one on each side, while Orestes dismounted. He stood for a moment with his hand on the horse's neck. "A good friend you have been, Bucephalus," he muttered. "May the gods send just punishment on any man who dares mistreat you!" Then with a quick look at the two trainers the slave went over and stood at his master's side.

"Get on his back and put him through his paces," the king ordered one of his trainers.

But this was easier said than done, for when the trainer made ready to mount, Bucephalus jerked his head angrily and strained at his bit. The strength of the two trainers was barely enough to hold him. Suddenly he reared straight up on his hind legs, almost pulling the two men off their feet.

"Easy, Bucephalus! Easy, good horse!" called Orestes, and leaving his master's side the slave hurried forward. "I will quiet him," he said to the trainers.

"Stay where you are, slave!" King Philip ordered sharply. "I must learn this horse's temper before I send him to my stables." Addressing his trainers he commanded that Bucephalus be mounted without further delay.

But King Philip's trainers, expert horsemen though they were, were not equal to this task. Bucephalus lunged and reared, kicking and biting at them if they so much as spoke to him. At last the king waved his hand in a gesture of disgust. "Take him away!" he cried angrily. "This horse is mad and altogether worthless. Turn him back to the slave. I would not give stable room to such a beast!"

The boy Alexander who had watched these proceedings with flushed face and flashing eye, now stepped quickly forward. "Wait!" he called, and with a scornful look at the two trainers he said in a loud, clear voice so that all might hear, "What an excellent horse they lost for want of address and boldness to manage him!"

King Philip turned sharply on his son. "Do you reproach those who are older than yourself," he said, "as if you knew more and were better able to manage the horse than they?"

Alexander answered boldly, "I could manage him better than the others do."

"And if you do not," said his father, "what will you forfeit for your rashness?"

Alexander did not hesitate. "I will pay," he answered, "the whole price of the horse."

In spite of his annoyance the king could not help laughing at the boy's bravado. And the company joined in the laugh.

But Alexander went swiftly to the horse's head, and motioning the trainers away he took the reins in his own hands. At once he turned Bucephalus about so that he was facing the sun, for he had noticed that the horse was shying nervously at his shadow on the ground. Then, stroking the sleek neck, Alexander talked to Bucephalus gently.

Little by little, the horse grew quiet. There was something in the touch of the boy's hand, something in the sound of his voice that gave Bucephalus confidence. He knew that here was someone he could trust.

With a quick leap Alexander was on the horse's back. Bucephalus threw his head up sharply and quivered with surprise. But his fear was gone. He pawed the ground, eager to be running free over the plain with this boy on his back.

And now Alexander spoke a word of command. Instantly Bucephalus bounded away and the boy did not try to stop him. Giving him his head he urged him to even greater speed. The king and his company looked on aghast, fearing that at any moment Alexander might be thrown to his death. But Orestes the slave smiled. "The lad has fine judgement with horses," he said. "Bucephalus is in good hands."

At last the horse slackened his pace and Alexander, turning him about, came riding back to the riding field, his face beaming with triumph. King Philip of Macedon was more proud at this moment than he had ever been before. This boy of sixteen was destined to conquer. The gods were with him!

Scarcely waiting for Alexander to dismount he threw his arms about the boy's neck and kissed him. "My son," he cried, "look you out a kingdom equal to and worthy of yourself! Macedon is too small for you!"

Little did King Philip think at the time how soon these

words would come true. Little did he dream that within four short years his son Alexander, mounted on this same Bucephalus, would ride out of Macedon at the head of a great army which was to conquer half the world.

Four short years – how quickly they passed. As the days went by Bucephalus grew to love the boy Alexander more and more. Eagerly he looked forward to those times when he could run, wild and free across the soft turf, the boy upon his back. This was what Bucephalus liked and it was what the boy liked. They understood each other, these two. They were friends.

But when the four short years were gone, Alexander was no longer a carefree boy. He was a king. For King Philip was dead, leaving his dream of empire unfinished. His son Alexander must finish it for him. The young king's boyhood days were now over, he must turn to war and conquest. It was a hard task but he was ready.

One day there gathered on the parade ground a company of horsemen. They were no ordinary horsemen, for they had shields and long sharp spears that glistened in the sunshine. These were fighting men.

A mighty cheer was lifted as young King Alexander approached mounted on his splendid horse Bucephalus. The fighting men lifted their spears in salute, and a moment later King Alexander and his army were on their way. Off they rode – to conquer a world.

Into far lands these Macedonians went. And always there was fighting and still more fighting. War! It was like a black cloud hiding the face of the sun. The world was turned into a world of hate and men forgot to be kind. There were years of hardship, suffering and bloodshed, but still Alexander's army marched on, conquering all before it.

King Philip's dream had come true, for Alexander was indeed the mightiest ruler in the world. His fame had reached into every land and wherever men talked of heroic deeds the names of the young king and his splendid horse were heard together. Alexander the Great and Bucephalus!

At first the horse had been frightened by the din of battle. The clang of weapons, the shouting of the soldiers, and the roaring and plunging of other horses round him had filled him with terror. But there was always the touch of his master's hand to quiet him, the sound of his master's voice to urge him on, and at last he grew accustomed to the tumult of war.

Through years of bitter fighting, Bucephalus served his master well, carrying him triumphantly through battle after battle. And with each victory the ambition of King Alexander increased. With each new conquest that he made, there came to him dreams of still greater conquest. He must go on and on, he told his men, until the whole world belonged to him.

But it takes a long time to conquer a world, and the life of a warhorse is hard. There came a day when Bucephalus could no longer go into battle. He was growing old.

Alexander was forced to leave him in camp far behind the fighting lines. Here the faithful horse was well cared for and happy, and each day the king came and talked to him, and Bucephalus would lower his head so that his master might stroke his nose and pull his silky ears. And sometimes he would thrust his muzzle forward and give King Alexander a playful shove, as he had once done with Orestes the slave in Thessaly.

Back in Thessaly the horse Bucephalus was not forgotten, and tales were told of the days when he was a colt and carried Orestes over the wide Thessalonian plains. The same flat plains still stretched away, and majestic Olympus, to the north, still raised its cloud-veiled summit. The years that had come and gone had brought little change to Thessaly.

"Orestes," said Philonicus one spring day, as again master and slave stood at the end of the green pasture, "do you remember the horse I sold for thirteen talents to King Philip of Macedon?"

"Yes, master," answered Orestes. "I shall not forget Bucephalus."

"Who would have dreamt," went on Philonicus, "that one day he would become the most famous horse in all the world? He is now almost as famous as the great Alexander himself."

"Bucephalus was always a good horse, master," Orestes said simply.

"Ay, a good horse," Philonicus repeated, turning away. "And thirteen talents was a good price, too. A handsome price, Orestes."

For a time the slave stood silent, and then walking slowly he went through the green pasture towards the little grove of trees. Midway of the field he paused and looked off at Mount Olympus. "A handsome price indeed," he said softly. "But if you had been mine, Bucephalus, not all the gold in Macedon could have bought you."

Dream Horses

All my life, I have dreamt of owning a pony: a cottage
in the country, with my black pony quietly grazing
in a field blazing with buttercups.

In "The Mud Pony", a Pawnee Indian boy longs to own
a pony like his friends. But his family is too poor.
Jess in "The Gift Horse" also knows her family
cannot afford to buy her a pony. Lennie in
"The Christmas Pony" longs for a pony so much, he is
prepared to have nothing else for Christmas.

Whatever the country or culture, the longing is always
the same and never goes away.

Luckily, amazing things do happen!

The Mud Pony
retold by Caron Lee Cohen

*In this traditional Native American tale, a boy and his
very unusual pony set out on a journey.*

THERE was once a poor boy in an Indian camp who
would watch by the creek as other boys watered
their ponies. More than anything, he longed for
a pony of his own.

So at last the boy crossed the creek, dug the wet earth
and shaped a pony out of mud. He gave it a white clay
face. He loved his mud pony. Every day he went to it and
took care of it as if it were real.

One day, while the boy was with his mud pony,
scouts rode into camp. "We've sighted buffalo several days'
journey west," they said. The people broke camp, for they
would starve in the months ahead if they didn't hunt the
buffalo. The boy's parents looked everywhere, but they
couldn't find him. Finally, they had to leave without him.

When the boy got back to camp, he saw that everyone was gone. "My people!" he cried out. "I will never find
you! I am all alone!" He wandered, heartsick and hungry,
around the empty camp, picking up scraps of dried meat
and a tattered old blanket someone had thrown away.
He ate, then huddled up in the blanket and cried himself
to sleep.

As he slept, he dreamt his mud pony was alive and
spoke to him: "My son, you are not alone. Mother Earth
has given me to you. I am part of her."

When the boy woke at daybreak in the empty camp,
he cried for his people. Then he went to his mud pony
and could hardly believe his eyes! The white-faced pony
was alive, tossing her mane and pawing the ground.

She spoke like the pony in his dream: "My son, you are
not alone. Mother Earth has given me to you. I am part of
her. You must do as I say, and someday you will be a chief
among your people. They are far away. Get on my back,
and I will take you to them. But do not try to guide me,
for I know where to go."

For three days they journeyed over the plains. The boy
was worn and hungry, but he would not give up; he let
the pony guide him.

Then at the third nightfall, the boy saw smoke curling
up from tepees in a camp. They had reached his people.

"Go and find your parents," said the pony. "But leave
them before dawn; it is not time yet for the others to see
you. I will be waiting in the hills. Now cover me with

the blanket to protect me from the rain, for I am part of
Mother Earth."

The boy went into the camp. He wandered among the
tepees until he found the smallest one. He went in and
threw dried grass into the fire, so a blaze went up. In the
fire's light he saw his mother and woke her.

"Here I am," he said.

She touched him and tears came into her eyes. Then
his father woke and marvelled at how the boy had found
them when they had gone so far away.

Before dawn the boy told his parents, "I must go now.
On my own." He left them, but from the hills he turned
and watched as the people broke camp to continue on
their way to the buffalo. At last they disappeared.

For three more days the boy and the pony journeyed
over the plains. The boy was weary and had no food at all,
but he kept on going.

Finally at the third nightfall, he saw a camp in the
distance. "There are your people," the pony said. "It is time
that you join them. Ride me into the camp."

The boy did. And all the people came out of their
tepees, astonished to see him.

A war chief invited him into a big tepee. There was
soup and dried meat and two buffalo horn spoons in a
wooden bowl. They ate together.

"Nawa, tiki!" the war chief saluted him. "You journeyed over strange land, starving and alone, and yet you
found us! You have a gift, a great power. And now you

must help our people. An enemy has attacked us on our way west, killing men, keeping us from reaching the buffalo. At daybreak you must join us in battle."

When the boy left the big tepee, he trembled. But the pony spoke to him: "My son, do not be afraid. For I am part of Mother Earth. And the enemy's arrows can never pierce the earth. Put earth all over your body, and you will not be hurt."

At daybreak he covered his body with earth and rode the pony straight into the fight. There was a fierce battle, but he led his people to victory. At last the people were free for the hunt, and the boy on the white-faced pony showed the way, capturing more buffalo than any of the grown men.

Years passed, and always the boy let his pony guide him. Always he was a powerful leader. Finally, he was made a chief! As a chief, he had a corral full of fine horses, but the white-faced pony was his great gift. He tied many eagle feathers into her mane and tail. And every nightfall he carefully covered her with a blanket to protect her from rain.

Then one night while he slept the pony came to him in a dream: "My son, now you are a chief among your people, a chief with the power of Mother Earth. It is Mother Earth who gives you the power, and not I. I am part of her, and it is time that I go back to her. You must let me go."

The chief got up in the dark and went to his pony. She

pawed the ground and tossed her mane in the wind. "Take my blanket," she said. He did. Then he went to his tepee.

Just before daybreak, he woke to shrill winds and rushing rain. He ran to his corral, and looked everywhere for his white-faced pony. He couldn't find her.

Then as the morning light broke over the wet earth, the chief saw a patch of white clay. And through the wind, he heard a voice: "I am here, your Mother Earth. You are not alone!"

The Gift Horse
June Crebbin

Jess dreams of owning a pony. Every week she scours the pony sales column in her local newspaper, even though she has no money. And no one ever gives ponies away, do they?

"FOR SALE: chestnut mare, brilliant jumper, £1,200."

If only.

I lay on my bed, scanning the Horse and Rider column of our weekly paper.

"Bay gelding, lively ride, £850."

I could handle that. The ride, not the money, I hasten to say. None of them was remotely within my means. My means being my pocket money, which was completely taken up paying towards my riding lessons.

But I had my dreams.

I read on.

"Black Shetland pony…"

Forget it. I know I'm small for my age, but not that small.

"Attractive blue roan, 14 hh…"

That was more like it.

I sighed. I read on to the Wanted section. Maybe this would be the day that someone had put: "WANTED, confident young rider to exercise stunning Appaloosa while owner at boarding school."

I should be so lucky. Most of the "wanted" was along the lines of grazing or stabling.

Maybe I should put in my own advertisement: "WANTED – a pony, any colour, any character, good home provided…"

After all, we were leaving our flat-above-the-shop for a country cottage. And it actually had a field behind it. A *perfect* home for a pony.

Downstairs, dinner was well on the way. Our last Sunday dinner in this house.

"Five minutes, Jess," Mum yelled up the stairs. "And the table still needs setting."

I turned back to the Horse and Rider column.

"LOVING OWNER required for GREY WELSH PONY."

I liked Welsh ponies.

"Sweet temperament."

Everyone liked those.

"Free to good home."

"Where's the fire?" Dad said, wisely leaping back as I came hurtling downstairs.

I thrust the newspaper under his nose.

"FREE!" I shouted. "FREE!"

I jabbed the phone number beneath the ad.

What if it was already too late?

I grabbed the phone.

"Hang on," said Dad, "I know this number."

I stared.

"It's old Mrs Spinetti."

It didn't sound very likely.

"I ring this number every week," said Dad. "Or I did. To get her order."

Dad's a greengrocer. He delivers to old and valued customers.

I cleared my throat. "And does she really...?" I began. I couldn't finish.

"Fancy her giving that pony away."

"Dad!"

"You've got it wrong," said Mum, coming to have a look. "She can't be *giving* it away."

"It says FREE!" I shrieked.

And then Dad said it. "You certainly don't look a gift horse in the mouth."

He knew how much I wanted a pony. He never made fun of me. And he didn't have to explain that money was tight. The new supermarket next door had brought our trade almost to a standstill. Dad had been really bitter about it, and worried. But then they'd wanted to extend their car park, and made him an offer he couldn't refuse. So we were off to the country with a brand-new van – a mobile shop.

And maybe a pony.

*   *   *

"There might be a catch," warned Dad on the way. "Even Mrs Spinetti may not be that kind and generous."

I crossed my fingers on both hands and prayed that Mrs Spinetti was the dearest, kindest, sweetest old lady this side of the Pennines.

"What's the pony like?" I asked. "You've never said. How old is it?"

An awful thought struck me. Maybe it was ancient and that was why Mrs Spinetti was giving it away. Maybe she wanted a good *retirement* home.

"All I know," said Dad, "is that one day, just after her husband died, Mrs Spinetti arrived home from Bakewell market with a pony. She takes it shopping and all sorts."

"Shopping?" I said. "A pony?"

I tried to imagine a little old lady popping down to the shops astride a pony with panniers flapping.

"Is it a mare or a gelding?" I said. "What's its name?"

Dad didn't know.

Misty. That would be good for a grey. Or Smoky. Or better still, Starlight. I really liked Starlight. Star, for when we were alone together, galloping across the dales, but in the showring … "And now we have Miss Jessica Brown and her pony Starlight." That sounded great.

Dad turned into a street of terraced houses in the middle of Allerton.

I wondered where Mrs Spinetti kept Starlight. It certainly couldn't be here.

"There she is!" said Dad.

A shortish lady in trousers and a brightly coloured shirt stood on a doorstep, waving. Not to us. To another car just pulling away.

Someone had beaten us to it. I tried to tell Dad but he was concentrating on parking.

"Well," said Mrs Spinetti when we got out of the car. "What a nice surprise!"

She ushered us in and we followed her through to the kitchen.

"Oh dear," said Dad, "we're interrupting your meal." There was a lovely smell of dinner and the table was laid.

"Don't worry," said Mrs Spinetti. She had a kind smile. "Why don't you stay?"

Of course, Dad said thank you, but our dinner would be waiting at home; we had just come about the pony but we could easily come back later.

"Has the pony gone?" I asked, but Mrs Spinetti was asking if we'd like a cup of tea.

We sat down.

"Would you prefer lemonade?" she said, turning to me.

Tea, lemonade, dishwater, what did I care! But I said, yes, please, she could pour me a glass, which she did. Then she poured Dad's tea and dished up her dinner. Finally, she lifted the empty washing-up bowl out of the sink, filled it with boiled potatoes, carrots and brussels sprouts, and put it on the table.

"He does enjoy his Sunday dinner," said Mrs Spinetti.

Who? I thought. A vegetarian giant? Mr Spinetti? But

then I remembered Dad telling me Mr Spinetti had died.

Mrs Spinetti opened the back door.

"Charlie!" she called. She clicked her tongue. "Come on, Charlie. Dinner time."

And into the kitchen stepped a pony.

Just his head and shoulders at first, then the rest. A middle-size, grey pony. His dappled coat, more light than dark, was like silver. His mane was almost white.

He swivelled his hindquarters past the sink, past the cooker. Mrs Spinetti shut the door, and he swivelled back. It was so neat. You could see it wasn't the first time he'd done it.

He lowered his head into the washing-up bowl, and ate.

I realized my mouth was open – and shut it. I looked at Dad. He was concentrating very hard on sipping his tea.

Luckily Mrs Spinetti was still chattering away: about Charlie (I ask you, what sort of a name is Charlie?); about her daughter who lived in Wapping and wanted her to go and live there too.

"It's my aches and pains," she said. "They're not getting any better." She patted Charlie's neck. "I just want to find him a good home."

"And have you?" I broke out. "Has Charlie gone yet?"

Mrs Spinetti looked at me. Clearly, she thought I was mad. Charlie hadn't gone: he was standing just the other side of the table!

"I mean..." I began.

"Has anyone offered him a home yet?" said Dad.

"Oh, yes," said Mrs Spinetti. "People have been coming all morning."

My heart sank.

"But they wouldn't agree," went on Mrs Spinetti.

Dad and I exchanged glances. I nodded my head so hard, I felt dizzy. *I'd* agree. I'd agree to anything.

"Wouldn't agree?" said Dad.

"Never to sell him," said Mrs Spinetti. "I can't bear to think of him being handed on. I wouldn't know he was all right, would I?"

I couldn't look at Dad then. Everyone knows that when you outgrow your first pony, you have to sell it in order to buy the next.

"I see," said Dad. He said he quite understood, he had every sympathy. I felt the chance of Charlie and me getting together slipping further and further away.

I couldn't just give up.

"*I* agree!" I burst out.

Dad stopped. He wasn't pleased. "I know how you feel, Jess, but it isn't that simple."

"It is," I said. "Here's Charlie and here's me and you know we can give him a good home."

Dad didn't argue about that.

"This might be my only chance to have a pony at all," I said. "He's a gift. And you know what you said – don't look a gift horse in the mouth!"

The Christmas Pony

Lincoln Steffens

*During the weeks before Christmas, excitement mounts.
So it is with Lennie, but will it be the best or the
worst Christmas he has ever known?*

WHAT interested me in our new neighbourhood was not the school, nor the room I was to have in the new house all to myself, but the stable which was built at the back of the house. My father let me direct the making of a stall, a little smaller than the other stalls, for my pony, and I prayed and hoped, and my sister Lou believed, that that meant that I would get the pony, perhaps for Christmas. I pointed out to her that there were three other stalls and no horses at all. This I said in order that she should answer it. She could not. My father, sounded out, said that someday we might have horses and a cow; meanwhile a stall could be kept clean and ready for the pony. I gave up reasoning, then. I knew. I had my horses and a cow; meanwhile a stable added to the value of a house. "Someday" is a pain to a boy who lives in and knows only "now". My good little sisters, to comfort me, remarked that Christmas was coming, but Christmas was always coming and grown-ups were always talking about it, asking you what you wanted and then giving you what they wanted you to have.

Though everybody knew what I wanted, I told them all again. My mother knew that I told God, too, every night. I wanted a pony, and to make sure they understood, I declared that I wanted nothing else.

"Nothing but a pony?" my father asked.

"Nothing," I said.

"Not even a pair of high boots?"

That was hard. I did want boots, but I stuck to the pony. "No, not even boots."

"Nor candy? There ought to be something to fill your stocking with, and Santa Claus can't put a pony into a stocking."

That was true, and he couldn't lead a pony down the chimney either. But no. "All I want is a pony," I said. "If I can't have a pony, give me nothing, nothing."

Now, I had been looking myself for the pony I wanted, going to sales stables, enquiring of horsemen, and I had seen several that would do. My father let me "try" them. I tried so many ponies that I was learning fast to sit a horse. I chose several, but my father always found some fault with them. I was in despair. When Christmas was at hand I had given up all hope of a pony, and on Christmas Eve I hung up my stocking along with my sisters', of whom, by the way, I now had three.

I speculated on what I'd get. I hung up the biggest stocking I had, and we all went reluctantly to bed to wait until morning. Not to sleep; not right away. We were told that we must not only sleep promptly, we must not wake up until seven-thirty – if we did, we must not go to the fireplace for our Christmas presents. Impossible.

We did sleep that night, but we woke up at 6 a.m. We lay in our beds and debated through the open doors whether to obey until, say, half past six. Then we bolted. I don't know who started it, but there was a rush. We all disobeyed; we raced to disobey and get first to the fireplace in the front room downstairs. And there they were, the gifts, all sorts of wonderful things, mixed-up piles of presents; only, as I disentangled the mess, I saw that my stocking was empty; it hung limp; not a thing in it; and under and around it – nothing. My sisters had knelt down, each by her pile of gifts; they were squealing with delight, until they looked up and saw me standing there in my nightgown with nothing. They left their piles to come to me and look with me at my empty place. Nothing. They felt my stocking: nothing.

I don't remember whether I cried at that moment, but my sisters did. They ran with me back to my bed, and there we all cried until I became indignant. That helped some. I got up, dressed, and driving my sisters away,

I went alone out into the yard, down to the stable, and there, all by myself, I wept. My mother came out to me by and by; she found me in my pony stall, sobbing on the floor, and she tried to comfort me. But I heard my father outside; he had come part way with her, and she was having some sort of angry quarrel with him. She tried to comfort me; besought me to come to breakfast. I could not; I wanted no comfort and no breakfast. She left me and went on into the house with sharp words for my father.

I don't know what kind of breakfast the family had. My sisters said it was "awful". They were ashamed to enjoy their own toys. They came to me, and I was rude. I ran away from them. I went around to the front of the house, sat down on the steps, and, the crying over, I ached. I was wronged, I was hurt – I can feel now what I felt then, and I am sure that if one could see the wounds upon our hearts, there would be found still upon mine a scar from that terrible Christmas morning. And my father, the practical joker, he must have been hurt, too, a little. I saw him looking out of the window. He was watching me or something for an hour or two, drawing back the curtain ever so little lest I catch him, but I saw his face, and I think I can see now the anxiety upon it, the worried impatience.

After I don't know how long, surely an hour or two, I was brought to the climax of my agony by the sight of a man riding a pony down the street, a pony and a brand-new saddle; the most beautiful saddle I ever saw, and it was a boy's saddle; the man's feet were not in the stirrups;

his legs were too long. The outfit was perfect; it was the realization of all my dreams, the answer to all my prayers. A fine new bridle, with a light curb bit. And the pony! As he drew near, I saw that the pony was really a small horse – what we called an Indian pony – a bay, with black mane and tail, and one white foot and a white star on his forehead. For such a horse as that I would have given, I could have given, anything.

But the man, a dishevelled fellow with a blackened eye and a fresh-cut face, came along, reading the numbers on the houses, and, as my hopes – my impossible hopes – rose, he looked at our door and passed by, he and the pony, and the saddle and the bridle. Too much. I fell upon the steps, and having wept before, I broke now into such a flood of tears that I was a floating wreck when I heard a voice.

"Say, kid," it said, "do you know a boy named Lennie Steffens?"

I looked up. It was the man on the pony, back again, at our horse block.

"Yes," I spluttered through my tears. "That's me."

"Well," he said, "then this is your horse. I've been looking all over for you and your house. Why don't you put your number where it can be seen?"

"Get down," I said, running out to him.

He went on saying something about "ought to have got here at seven o'clock; told me to bring the nag here and tie him to your post and leave him for you. But I got into a

68

drunk – and a fight – and a hospital – and—"

"Get down," I said.

He got down, and he boosted me up to the saddle. He offered to fit the stirrups to me, but I didn't want him to. I wanted to ride.

"What's the matter with you?" he said, angrily. "What you crying for? Don't you like the horse? He's a dandy, this horse. I know him of old. He's fine at cattle; he'll drive 'em alone."

I hardly heard, I could scarcely wait, but he persisted. He adjusted the stirrups, and then, finally, off I rode, slowly, at a walk, so happy, so thrilled, that I did not know what I was doing. I did not look back at the house or the man, I rode off up the street, taking note of everything – of the reins, of the pony's long mane, of the carved leather saddle. I had never known anything so beautiful. And mine! I was going to ride up past Miss Kay's house. But I noticed on the horn of the saddle some stains like raindrops, so I turned and trotted home, not to the house but to the stable. There was the family, father, mother, sisters, all working for me, all happy. They had been putting in place the tools of my new business: blankets, curry-comb, brush, pitchfork – everything, and there was hay in the loft.

"What did you come back so soon for?" somebody asked. "Why didn't you go on riding?"

I pointed to the stains. "I wasn't going to get my new saddle rained on," I said. And my father laughed. "It isn't raining," he said. "Those are not raindrops."

"They are tears," my mother gasped, and she gave my father a look which sent him off to the house. Worse still, my mother offered to wipe away the tears still running out of my eyes. I gave her such a look as she had given him, and she went off after my father, drying her own tears. My sisters remained and we all unsaddled the pony, put on his halter, led him to his stall, tied and fed him. It began really to rain; so all the rest of that memorable day we curried and combed that pony. The girls plaited his mane, forelock and tail, while I pitchforked hay to him and curried and brushed, curried and brushed. For a change we brought him out to drink; we led him up and down, blanketed like a racehorse; we took turns at that. But the best, the most inexhaustible fun, was to clean him. When we went reluctantly to our midday Christmas dinner, we all smelt of horse, and my sisters had to wash their faces and hands. I was asked to, but I wouldn't until my mother bade me look in the mirror. Then I washed up – quick. My face was caked with the muddy lines of tears that had coursed over my cheeks to my mouth. Having washed away that shame, I ate my dinner, and as I ate I grew hungrier and hungrier. It was my first meal that day, and as I filled up on the turkey and the stuffing, the cranberries and the pies, the fruit and the nuts – as I swelled, I could laugh. My mother said I still choked and sobbed now and then, but I laughed, too; I saw and enjoyed my sisters' presents until I had to go out and attend to my pony, who was there, really and truly there, the promise, the beginning of a happy double life. And – I went and looked to make sure – there was the saddle, too, and the bridle.

But that Christmas, which my father had planned so carefully, was it the best or the worst I ever knew? He often asked me that; I never could answer as a boy. I think now that it was both. It covered the whole distance from broken-hearted misery to bursting happiness – too fast. A grown-up could hardly have stood it.

From the Horse's Mouth

The most successful horse-and-rider partnerships must,
I believe, be based on trust. It's a two-way thing.
We talk about our horse or pony "listening" to us: to the
movements of our body, our legs, our hands.
Horses usually respond to firm but kind handling;
they learn to trust our judgement.
But we also need to understand them: how bored they
may feel about endless winter days stuck in a stable; how
much reassurance they may need in a new situation.

In "War Horse" we hear how Joey feels about his new life
straight from the horse's mouth: how much he misses Albert
who brought him up; how harsh he finds his new trainer.

In "Black Beauty", set in the time when horses were
the main means of transport, we learn from Beauty about
his early life at the Hall and how, one stormy day,
his master is sensible enough to "listen" to him!

Sometimes, horses know best!

War Horse
Michael Morpurgo

It is the summer of 1914. War has been declared between England and Germany. Horses are needed for the cavalry. Deep in the Devon countryside, Joey, a beautiful red bay, who has only known the life of a working farm, is bought by the army.

IN the few short weeks before I went off to war I was to be changed from a working farmhorse into a cavalry mount. It was no easy transformation, for I resented deeply the tight disciplines of the riding school and the hard hot hours out on manoeuvres on the Plain. Back at home with Albert I had revelled in the long rides along the lanes and over the fields, and the heat and the flies had not seemed to matter; I had loved the aching days of ploughing and harrowing alongside Zoey, but that was because there had been a bond between us of trust and devotion. Now there were endless tedious hours circling the school. Gone was the gentle snaffle bit that I was so used to, and in its place was an uncomfortable, cumbersome Weymouth that snagged the corners of my mouth and infuriated me beyond belief.

But it was my rider that I disliked more than anything in my new life. Corporal Samuel Perkins was a hard, gritty little man, an ex-jockey whose only pleasure in life seemed to be the power he could exert over a horse. He was universally feared by all troopers and horses alike. Even the officers, I felt, went in trepidation of him; for he knew, it seemed, all there was to know about horses and had the experience of a lifetime behind him. And he rode hard and heavy-handed. With him the whip and the spurs were not just for show.

He would never beat me or lose his temper with me, indeed sometimes when he was grooming me I think maybe he quite liked me and I certainly felt for him a degree of respect, but this was based on fear and not love. In my anger and unhappiness I tried several times to throw him off but never succeeded. His knees had a grip of iron and he seemed instinctively to know what I was about to do.

My only consolation in those early days of training were the visits of Captain Nicholls every evening to the stables. He alone seemed to have the time to come and talk to me as Albert had done before. Sitting on an upturned bucket in the corner of my stable, a sketchbook on his knees, he would draw me as he talked. "I've done a few sketches of you now," he said one evening, "and when I've finished this one I'll be ready to paint a picture of you. It won't be Stubbs – it'll be better than Stubbs because Stubbs never had a horse as beautiful as you to paint. I can't take it with me to France – no point, is there? So I'm going to send it off to your friend Albert, just so that he'll know that I meant what I said when I promised I would look after you." He kept looking up and down at me as he worked and I longed to tell him how much I wished he would take over my training himself and how hard the Corporal was and how my sides hurt and my feet hurt. "To be honest with you, Joey, I hope this war will be over before he's old enough to join us because – you mark my words – it's going to be nasty, very nasty indeed. Back in the mess they're all talking about how they'll set about Jerry, how the cavalry will smash through them and throw them clear back to Berlin before Christmas. It's just Jamie and me, we're the only ones that don't agree, Joey. We have our doubts, I can tell you that. We have our doubts. None of them in there seem to have heard of machine-guns and artillery. I tell you, Joey, one machine-gun operated right could wipe out an entire squadron of the best cavalry in the world – German or British. I mean, look what happened to the Light Brigade at Balaclava when they took on the Russian guns – none of them seem to remember that. And the French learnt the lesson in the Franco-Prussian War. But you can't say anything to them, Joey. If you do, they call you defeatist, or some such rubbish. I honestly think that some of them in there only want to win this war if the cavalry can win it."

He stood up, tucked his sketchbook under his arm and came over towards me and tickled me behind the ears. "You like that, old son, don't you? Below all that fire and brimstone you're a soppy old date at heart. Come to think of it we have a lot in common you and I. First, we don't much like it here and would rather be somewhere else. Second, we've neither of us ever been to war – never even heard a shot fired in anger, have we? I just hope I'm up to it when the time comes – that's what worries me more than anything, Joey. Because, I tell you, and I haven't even told Jamie this – I'm frightened as hell, so you'd better have enough courage for the two of us."

A door banged across the yard and I heard the familiar sound of boots, crisp on the cobbles. It was Corporal Samuel Perkins passing along the lines of stables on his evening rounds, stopping at each one to check until at last he came to mine. "Good evening, sir," he said, saluting smartly. "Sketching again?"

"Doing my best, Corporal," said Captain Nicholls. "Doing my best to do him justice. Is he not the finest mount in the entire squadron? I've never seen a horse so well put together as he is. Have you?"

"Oh, he's special enough to look at, sir," said the Corporal of Horse. Even his voice put my ears back, there was a thin, acid tone to it that I dreaded. "I grant you that, but looks aren't everything, are they, sir? There's always more to a horse than meets the eye, isn't that right, sir? How shall I put it, sir?"

"However you like, Corporal," said Captain Nicholls somewhat frostily, "but be careful what you say for that's my horse you're speaking about, so take care."

"Let's say I feel he has a mind of his own. Yes, let's put it that way. He's good enough out on manoeuvres – a real stayer, one of the very best – but inside the school, sir, he's a devil, and a strong devil too. Never been properly schooled, sir, you can tell that. Farm-horse he is and farm trained. If he's to make a cavalry horse, sir, he'll have to learn to accept the disciplines. He has to learn to obey instantly and instinctively. You don't want a prima donna under you when the bullets start flying."

"Fortunately, Corporal," said Captain Nicholls. "Fortunately this war will be fought out of doors and not indoors. I asked you to train Joey because I think you are the best man for the job – there's no one better in the squadron. But perhaps you should ease up on him just a bit. You've got to remember where he came from. He's a willing soul – he just needs a bit of gentle persuasion, that's all. But keep it gentle, Corporal, keep it gentle. I don't want him soured. This horse is going to carry me through the war and, with any luck, out the other side of it. He's special to me, Corporal, you know that. So make sure you look after him as if he was your own, won't you? We leave for France in under a week now. If I had the time I'd be schooling him on myself, but I'm far too busy trying to turn troopers into mounted infantry. A horse may carry you through, Corporal, but he can't do your fighting for you. And there's some of them still think they'll only be needing their sabres when they get out there. Some of them really believe that flashing their sabres around will frighten Jerry all the way home. I tell you they have got to learn to shoot straight – we'll all have to learn to shoot straight if we want to win this war."

"Yes, sir," said the Corporal with a new respect in his voice. He was more meek and mild now than I had ever seen him.

"And Corporal," said Captain Nicholls walking towards the stable door, "I'd be obliged if you'd feed Joey up somewhat, he's lost a bit of condition, gone back a bit I'd say. I shall be taking him out myself on final manoeuvres in two or three days and I want him fit and shining. He's to look the best in the squadron."

It was only in that last week of my military education that I began at last to settle into the work. Corporal Samuel Perkins seemed less harsh towards me after that evening. He used the spurs less and gave me more rein.

We did less work now in the school and more formation work on the open plains outside the camp. I took the Weymouth bit more readily now and began to play with it between my teeth as I had always done with the snaffle. I began to appreciate the good food and the grooming and the buffing up, all the unending attention and care that was devoted to me. As the days passed I began to think less and less of the farm and old Zoey and of my early life. But Albert, his face and his voice stayed clear in my mind despite the unerring routine of the work that was turning me imperceptibly into an army horse.

By the time Captain Nicholls came to take me out on those last manoeuvres before we went to war I was already quite resigned to, even contented in my new life. Dressed now in field service marching order, Captain Nicholls weighed heavy on my back as the entire regiment moved out onto Salisbury Plain. I remember mostly the heat and the flies that day for there were hours of standing about in the sun waiting for things to happen. Then with the evening sun spreading and dying along the flat horizon the entire regiment lined up in echelon for the charge, the climax of our last manoeuvres.

The order was given to draw swords and we walked forward. As we waited for the bugle calls the air was electric with anticipation. It passed between every horse and his rider, between horse and horse, between trooper and trooper. I felt inside me a surge of such excitement that I found it difficult to contain myself. Captain Nicholls was leading his troop and alongside him rode his friend Captain Jamie Stewart on a horse I had never seen before. He was a tall, shining black stallion. As we walked forward I glanced up at him and caught his eye. He seemed to acknowledge it briefly. The walk moved into a trot and

then into a canter. I heard the bugles blow and caught sight of his sabre pointing over my right ear. Captain Nicholls leant forward in the saddle and urged me into a gallop. The thunder and the dust and the roar of men's voices in my ears took a hold of me and held me at a pitch of exhilaration I had never before experienced. I flew over the ground way out ahead of the rest of them except for one. The only horse to stay with me was the shining black stallion. Although nothing was said between Captain Nicholls and Captain Stewart, I felt it was suddenly important that I should not allow this horse to get ahead of me. One look told me that he felt the same, for there was a grim determination in his eyes and his brow was furrowed with concentration. When we overran the "enemy" position it was all our riders could do to bring us to a halt, and finally we stood nose to nose, blowing and panting with both captains breathless with exertion.

"You see, Jamie, I told you so," said Captain Nicholls, and there was such pride in his voice as he spoke. "This is the horse I was telling you about – found in deepest Devon – and if we had gone on much longer your Topthorn would have been struggling to stay with him. You can't deny it."

Topthorn and I looked warily at each other at first. He was half a hand or more higher than me, a huge sleek horse that held his head with majestic dignity. He was the first horse I had ever come across that I felt could challenge me for strength, but there was also a kindness in his eye that held no threat for me.

"My Topthorn is the finest mount in this regiment, or any other," said Captain Jamie Stewart. "Joey might be faster, and all right, I'll grant he looks as good as any horse I've ever seen pulling a milk float, but there's no one to match my Topthorn for stamina – why he could have gone on for ever and ever. He's an eight horsepower horse, and that's a fact."

On the way back to the barracks that evening the two officers debated the virtues of their respective horses, whilst Topthorn and I plodded along shoulder to shoulder, heads hanging – our strength sapped by the sun and the long gallop. We were stabled side by side that night, and again on the boat the next day we found ourselves together in the bowels of the converted liner that was to carry us off to France and away to the war.

Black Beauty
Anna Sewell

Black Beauty is a handsome, good-tempered horse, quiet and well mannered, and always ready to do his master's bidding.

ONE day late in the autumn, my master had a long journey to go on business. I was put into the dog-cart, and John went with his master. I always liked to go in the dog-cart, it was so light, and the high wheels ran along so pleasantly. There had been a great deal of rain, and now the wind was very high, and blew the dry leaves across the road in a shower. We went along merrily till we came to the toll-bar, and the low wooden bridge. The river banks were rather high, and the bridge, instead of rising, went across just level, so that in the middle, if the river was full, the water would be nearly up to the woodwork and planks; but as there were good substantial rails on each side, people did not mind it.

The man at the gate said the river was rising fast, and he feared it would be a bad night. Many of the meadows were under water, and in one low part of the road the water was halfway up to my knees; the bottom was good, and the master drove gently, so it was no matter.

When we got to the town, of course, I had a good wait, but as the master's business engaged him a long time, we did not start for home till rather late in the afternoon. The wind was then much higher, and I heard the master say to John he had never been out in such a storm; and so I thought, as we went along the skirts of a wood, where the great branches were swaying about like twigs, and the rushing sound was terrible.

"I wish we were well out of this wood," said my master.

"Yes, sir," said John, "it would be rather awkward if one of these branches came down upon us."

The words were scarcely out of his mouth, when there was a groan, and a crack, and a splitting sound, and tearing crashing down amongst the other trees came an oak, torn up by the roots, and it fell right across the road just before us. I will never say I was not frightened, for I was. I stopped still, and I believe I trembled; of course, I did not turn around or run away; I was not brought up to that. John jumped out and was in a moment at my head.

"That was a very near touch," said my master. "What's to be done now?"

"Well, sir, we can't drive over that tree nor yet round it;

there will be nothing for it but to go back to the four crossways, and that will be a good six miles before we get round to the wooden bridge again; it will make us late, but the horse is fresh."

So back we went, and round by the crossroads; but by the time we got to the bridge it was very nearly dark, we could just see that the water was over the middle of it; but as that happened sometimes when the floods were out, master did not stop. We were going along at a good pace, but the moment my feet touched the first part of the bridge, I felt sure there was something wrong. I dare not go forward, and I made a dead stop. "Go on, Beauty," said my master, and he gave me a touch with the whip, but I dare not stir; he gave me a sharp cut, I jumped, but I dare not go forward.

"There's something wrong, sir," said John, and he sprang out of the dog-cart and came to my head and looked all about. He tried to lead me forward, "Come on, Beauty, what's the matter?" Of course, I could not tell him, but I knew very well that the bridge was not safe.

Just then the man at the toll-gate on the other side ran out of the house, tossing a torch about like one mad.

"Hoy, hoy, hoy, halloo, stop!" he cried.

"What's the matter?" shouted my master.

"The bridge is broken in the middle and part of it is carried away; if you come on you'll be into the river."

"Thank God!" said my master.

"You Beauty!" said John and took the bridle and gently

turned me round to the right-hand road by the river-side. The sun had set some time, the wind seemed to have lulled off after that furious blast which tore up the tree. It grew darker and darker, stiller and stiller. I trotted quietly along, the wheels hardly making a sound on the soft road. For a good while neither master nor John spoke, and then master began in a serious voice. I could not understand much of what they said, but I found they thought if I had gone on as the master wanted me, most likely the bridge would have given way under us, and horse, chaise, master, and man would have fallen into the river; and as the current was flowing very strongly, and there was no light and no help at hand, it was more than likely we should all have been drowned. Master said, God had given men reason, by which they could find out things for themselves, but He had given animals knowledge which did not depend on reason, and which was much more prompt and perfect in its way, and by which they had often saved the lives of men. John had many stories to tell of dogs and horses, and the wonderful things they had done; he thought people did not value their animals half enough, nor make friends of them as they ought to do. I am sure he makes friends of them if ever a man did.

At last we came to the Park gates, and found the gardener looking out for us. He said that mistress had been in a dreadful way ever since dark, fearing some accident had happened, and that she had sent James off on Justice, the roan cob, towards the wooden bridge to make enquiry after us.

We saw a light at the hall door and at the upper windows, and as we came up mistress ran out, saying, "Are you really safe, my dear? Oh! I have been so anxious, fancying all sorts of things. Have you had no accident?"

"No, my dear; but if your Black Beauty had not been wiser than we were, we should all have been carried down the river at the wooden bridge." I heard no more, as they went into the house, and John took me to the stable. Oh! what a good supper he gave me that night, a good bran mash and some crushed beans with my oats, and such a thick bed of straw, and I was glad of it, for I was tired.

Horses in Danger

Nowadays we do our utmost to make sure that horses and ponies are never put in danger. There are societies to protect them and laws forbidding ill-treatment.

In the past, however, it was often a different story. In "I Rode a Horse of Milk-White Jade", set in fourteenth-century Mongolia, the great Kublai Khan simply stole horses from peace-loving tribesmen to use in his many wars.

Travelling by sea was particularly hazardous in the sixteenth century, as the live cargo in "Misty of Chincoteague" discovers.

In "Pony in the Dark", set in nineteenth-century Britain, Storm is in constant danger working below ground in a coalmine.

And, finally, in "Unicorn", a timeless tale, a young silvery-white unicorn is in danger of its life.

I Rode a Horse of Milk White Jade
Diane Lee Wilson

Oyuna lives on the Mongolian steppes, a member of the Kerait tribe, who travel the land with their herd of horses. While still a baby, Oyuna's foot is accidentally crushed by a black mare. Yet, as she grows, Oyuna teaches herself to ride and at last is allowed her own horse. Strangely, she feels compelled to choose a certain white mare, Bayan, who, though beautiful, is old and lame. One day, Oyuna, now living with Shuraa, her new stepmother, and two stepbrothers, climbs a hillside outside their camp. In the distance, a host of horsemen is galloping towards her.

SOLDIERS! Nearly a hundred mounted soldiers, each carrying a round shield, so that they moved across the steppe as if the great solid walls of Karakorum marched. They were approaching fast, intent, I guessed, on taking our small *ail* by surprise. I had to warn the others!

Jumping to my feet, I slid and hopped in a rush down the hillside.

But the dogs in camp had already spotted the strangers and now joined voices in their own yipping alert. As I limped closer to the cluster of *gers* I saw the men of my ail gathering the women and young children and shoving them into the small safety of the felt shelters. My eyes and ears were so full of the noisy confusion, I barely noticed the strong grasp of my father's hand upon my arm, steering me forcefully toward our ger. With a push I was shoved inside, nearly stumbling over the pile of a wailing Shuraa clutching her two sons onto what little lap her swollen belly allowed.

Against Shuraa's weak cries of protest I turned and crawled back toward the door flap, pushing it out just enough to lay an eye against the slit and watch, panting heavily, what was happening.

The wind blew stronger and stronger, sending young leaves and bits of grass skittering through our camp. It blasted into the approaching line of soldiers, lifting the flaps of their black *dels* up and down like so many birds' wings. The riders had appeared so suddenly, in fact, that it seemed almost as if they had dropped, in one great flock, from the sky. The men and older boys of our ail gathered in a small knot at the farthest ger, bracing themselves against the wind and waiting. In the next instant the soldiers were upon them, half of the flock settling around the men, spears pointing, holding them helpless. The other half wheeled off toward the horses, waving their arms and shouting wildly.

And then my heart swelled in my throat as I began to understand. The soldiers were after our horses! They must be the Khan's soldiers, then, for I knew that he could take whatever horses he needed from his people. But in my twelve years I had never seen soldiers within our own camp.

Our herd, already nervous with the sudden arrival of the strange men and their horses, flung their tails into the air and took off. I do not like to admit this, but as I watched these soldiers run after our horses, I admired their skills in the saddle. Each rider and his mount worked as one, leaning into the herd and turning the panicked animals this way and that. Shouting and waving their arms, the riders circled the horses, gradually drawing the invisible noose tighter and smaller until the pack came to a stop, confused.

Then, dropping from the sky like a hawk, fell an *urga*, the herdsman's long pole with a leather loop at its end, around the neck of one quivering horse. Exhausted and scared, the horse, a tall, white-nosed bay belonging to an uncle, was dragged from the herd and hobbled. A dozen soldiers moved alongside it to guard against escape. Time after time, I watched the urga shoot through the air, settling around the neck of another of our horses. And I saw that the soldiers chose only the best. The brief gallop had proven which of our herd were truly the strongest and fastest.

Next the noose fell around the head of my father's old spotted stallion, but a close inspection after pulling him from the herd caused shaking heads and the urga's release. After all, even my father and I knew the old stallion had not many winters left. But one of the young sorrel mares my father had brought back from Karakorum was taken – and she with a lovely filly not more than ten days old at her side!

One by one, horse by horse, the urga settled over heads until thirty of our finest-bred horses stood hobbled apart from the herd. As the first group grew smaller and the new group grew larger, frantic neighs filled the air.

And then a horse's familiar scream shot through the clamour, so shrill that my own scream was drowned. For out of the herd had lunged Bayan, my white mare, with the urga tightening around her snowy neck. She tore along magnificently, plunging and bucking, while the rider tried in vain to bring her to a halt. Just as they entered the open steppe, another urga fell around her head. Restrained on both sides, Bayan reared and pawed the air. I had never seen her look so beautiful. Then she ducked her head and lashed out at one rider with both hind feet. Even at that great distance I saw the men point and laugh approvingly. "Spirit!" I heard one shout.

I couldn't believe it – any of it. That my lovely white mare was no longer lame – that she, my friend, was being so mistreated – that she was being taken away from me. "No, no, no!" I screamed over and over far out of earshot

of the soldiers. I watched in helpless horror as the two riders yanked Bayan towards the smaller herd, while she continued rearing and bucking tirelessly. It took two more men to fit hobbles around her front ankles, and when she knocked one onto his seat with a sharp kick, a back leg was tied snugly to the front pair. I watched through eyes brimming with tears as the soldiers tied more ropes around her, even haltering her to a horse already standing quietly. Bayan finally gave up resisting and stood quivering and nickering fitfully. I saw her looking around and I knew she was searching for me.

I was sobbing now, my shoulders heaving. The scene swam before my tear-filled eyes as in a terrible dream.

Sharp calls were exchanged between the soldiers guarding the men and the ones guarding the horses. Then the first group raised their spears. Swiftly, one after another, with just a threatening point into the chest of a helpless herdsman, new soldiers were added to the Khan's army. I saw three chosen, two uncles and a cousin, who bowed their heads and walked slowly toward their gers.

The commander of the soldiers then dismounted and stomped stiffly from ger to ger stooping and thrusting his head into each one. When he neared ours, I shrank away from the door flap and sat trembling, trying to stop my crying. And trying to think what I could do to save Bayan.

Shuraa was wailing wildly, clutching her two sons to her and rocking back and forth in a great jumble of flailing hands and legs. I watched numbly as the *tarag* bubbled out of its pot, spilling into the fire and sending up smelly clouds of steam. No one moved to stop it.

A dark head boldly pushed past the door flap, bringing with it a deep voice that bellowed, "Soldiers for the Khan's army!" Wide shoulders followed and soon the large, heavy body of the soldiers' leader swallowed up the remaining space in our ger. He carried in with him on his black uniform the pungent odour of sagebrush, of dung smoke and leather oil. When he lifted his head to look around I cringed at the thick, fleshy face, with its single black eyebrow digging a track across a bony brow.

Ignoring Shuraa's arms clasped around her two sons, the man closed his hairy hand around the small wrist of my older stepbrother. In one sharp motion the hand pulled the wrist upward, so that the boy's body had to follow, though it dangled weakly, like a lamb freshly killed for dinner.

"Here is a soldier, I think," the man snarled. "A puny one, but he will do."

"No, no!" screamed Shuraa, jumping to her feet and spilling her younger son off her lap. She propped her short body beneath her dangling son's limp shoulder. "He has a crippled leg – you will see. He can walk no more than a crawl." Thus supporting him, Shuraa bent over and pushed at her son's legs with one hand as if they were the wooden legs of a toy. Curious, the man released his grip. It was then that I saw Shuraa pinch her son, hard, behind the knee. He cried out and limped a painful step forward.

"See?" she said, glancing nervously into the hard face of the commander and pulling her son close into her arms. "See? It is my heartbreak to bear, not yours. You do not want a limping soldier."

The man merely glared at Shuraa. His hand reached out and grabbed the boy forward again. The fleshy face was thrust before the boy's wide eyes. "You may limp in the dirt, soldier, but you won't limp in the saddle. Pack your things. Now!" He jerked the boy's wrist to emphasize his point, then with a cursory glance around the ger, one that swept over my head, the large man turned and left. I heard him shout to his men to prepare to leave.

Shuraa was sobbing again in a helpless heap upon the rug, her two sons kneeling, foggy-eyed and unmoving, beside her.

I released in a rush the sobs I had reined in while the terrifying commander was in our ger. Head pressed upon my knees, I, too, swayed back and forth, crying out for the lovely white mare that was being taken from me.

I saw something glinting through my tears. Wiping a sleeve across my eyes, I blinked and bent forward. Lying at my feet on the rug was a small gold likeness of a winged horse with a girl on its back carrying flowers in her hands. Instantly I remembered the small black amulet in the palm of my grandmother, Echenkorlo. I reached for the gold figurine brought it close to my face and studied the curving form. A loop at the top, moulded into the design, told it was an adornment for a belt or a horse's harness.

And then the strangest thing! Holding that winged pendant in my palm, I felt a great calmness settle over me, like the calm that settles just before a storm, giving you a brief moment to prepare for the fury to follow. You scurry around gathering up this, pinning down that, never knowing whether you will even be alive in the morning. Clearly then, as I had at Karakorum, I heard the words in my head: *Now, now, now!* And I knew what to do.

Tightly clutching the gold ornament, I stood and, with the trembling fingers of one hand, quickly unfastened and slipped out of my del. One limping step and I was at the side of my older stepbrother, hastily unfastening his dark green del. He, too, was trembling, biting his lip and crying. He said nothing as I slipped the del from his limp arms and fastened it around my own body. I picked up his orange belt and knotted it around my waist, marking me a boy. Then I dropped the heavy ornament into an inner pocket.

Shuraa suddenly came alive. "No! You can't!" she cried. "You are just a girl. You're weak, crippled."

Wordlessly, but with great assurance, I stepped across her sprawling leg. Shuraa clawed at my hand and shouted, "They're killers, Oyuna! My own father died in the Khan's army. And my first husband. You don't know the danger!"

But there were so many noises buzzing in my head that I could not heed Shuraa. Halting before the cabinet that still held the stuffed doll with one leg dyed red, I stared. The doll leered back, taunting. *Bad luck*, it seemed to whisper through stained lips. Shuraa's words echoed: "You are just a girl. You're weak, crippled." I took a deep breath, picked up the doll, and cautiously laid it face down. I pulled a knife from the top drawer. Tipping my head to one side, I lifted the knife to my braid and, with a hard sawing motion, cut it off. Then I tucked the knife within my felt boot. From the wall I grabbed my father's fur-trimmed felt hat and pulled it down over my head, nearly hiding my face.

I reached under the bed and pulled out Echenkorlo's dust-covered leather pouch, slinging it across my shoulder. I dipped water into a spare pouch and strapped it around my shoulder as well, then stuffed a handful of dried mutton strips inside my del. Lifting my saddle in my arms, I stumbled under all the weight toward the door flap.

Bator was suddenly at my feet, rubbing his body around my legs, eager to follow. He usually trotted out a bit with me when I left on a ride.

"Not this time, Bator," I said, wishing I had a free hand to give him a final pat. "Better you stay inside." He meowed. I didn't look back.

Already the other new soldiers, all relatives of mine, were saddling their horses. Everywhere women were wailing. Not daring to glance to where my father stood, I carried my saddle straight toward the white mare. As I passed beneath the glare of the heavy-browed commander, he noted my limp and grunted, satisfied.

With my heart thumping, I lifted my saddle onto

Bayan, the horse I had never ridden. But there was that look in her eye again, the same twinkle promising adventure which I had trusted at Karakorum, and I knew now I was meant to ride her. With the bridle fitted upon her head and the girth tightened around her stomach, I quickly unknotted the hobbles and ropes. Then I stepped into the stirrup, swung my crippled leg over, and sat lightly upon her back. When the soldiers moved to release the hobbles from the horses they were stealing, I was already hidden among the other soldiers riding east. The morning wind blew straight into our faces, chilling our skin with its cold breath. Yet, tucking my face between collar and hat, I smiled. For seated upon Bayan's back I felt as if I had wings.

ail – a group of herdsmen and their families
travelling and camping together

del – a thick wraparound robe with a stiff,
stand-up collar; the traditional Mongolian garment

ger – a circular tent made of layers of felt
stretched over a wicker frame

tarag – a thin yogurt

Misty of Chincoteague
Marguerite Henry

A Spanish galleon is making its way to Peru with a cargo of ponies destined for the gold mines. But as the ship nears two small islands off the eastern coast of America, a storm breaks.

A WILD, ringing neigh shrilled up from the hold of the Spanish galleon. It was not the cry of an animal in hunger. It was a terrifying bugle. An alarm call.

The captain of the *Santo Cristo* strode the poop deck. "Cursed be that stallion!" he muttered under his breath as he stamped forward and back, forward and back.

Suddenly he stopped short. The wind! It was dying with the sun. It was spilling out of the sails, causing them to quiver and shake. He could feel his flesh creep with the sails. Without wind he could not get to Panama. And if he did not get there, and get there soon, he was headed for trouble. The Moor ponies to be delivered to the Viceroy of Peru could not be kept alive much longer. Their hay had grown musty. The water casks were almost empty. And now this sudden calm, this heavy warning of a storm.

He plucked nervously at his rusty black beard as if that would help him think. "We lie in the latitude of white squalls," he said, a look of vexation on his face. "When the wind does strike, it will strike with fury." His steps quickened. "We must shorten sail," he made up his mind.

Cupping his hands to his mouth, he bellowed orders: "Furl the topgallant sail! Furl the coursers and the main-topsail! Shorten the fore-topsail!"

The ship burst into action. From forward and aft all hands came running. They fell to work furiously, carrying out orders.

The captain's eyes were fixed on his men, but his thoughts raced ahead to the rich land where he was bound. In his mind's eye he could see the mule train coming to meet him when he reached land. He could see it snaking its way along the Gold Road from Panama to the seaport of Puerto Bello. He could almost feel the smooth, hard gold in the packs on the donkeys' backs.

His eyes narrowed greedily. "Gold!" he mumbled.

"Think of trading twenty ponies for their weight in gold!" He clasped his hands behind him and resumed his pacing and muttering. "The Viceroy of Peru sets great store by the ponies, and well he may. Without the ponies to work the mines, there will be no more gold." Then he clenched his fists. "We must keep the ponies alive!"

His thoughts were brought up sharply. That shrill horse call! Again it filled the air about him with a wild ring. His beady eyes darted to the lookout man in the crow's nest, then to the men on deck. He saw fear spread among the crew.

Meanwhile, in the dark hold of the ship, a small bay stallion was pawing the floor of his stall. His iron shoes with their sharp rims and turned-down heels threw a shower of sparks, and he felt strong charges of electricity. His nostrils flared. The moisture in the air! The charges of electricity! These were storm warnings – things he knew. Some inner urge told him he must get his mares to high land before the storm broke. He tried to escape, charging against the chest board of his stall again and again. He threw his head back and bugled.

From stalls beside him and from stalls opposite him, nineteen heads with small pointed ears peered out. Nineteen pairs of brown eyes whited. Nineteen young mares caught his anxiety. They, too, tried to escape, rearing and plunging, rearing and plunging.

But presently the animals were no longer hurling themselves. They were *being* hurled. The ship was pitching and tossing to the rising swell of the sea, flinging the ponies forward against their chest boards, backward against the ship's sides.

A cold wind spiralled down the hatch. It whistled and screamed above the rough voice of the captain. It gave way only to the deep *flump-flump* of the thunder.

The sea became a wildcat now, and the galleon her prey. She stalked the ship and drove her off her course. She slapped at her, rolling her victim from side to side. She knocked the spars out of her and used them to ram holes in her sides. She clawed the rudder from its sternpost and threw it into the sea. She cracked the ship's ribs as if they were brittle bones. Then she hissed and spat through the seams.

The pressure of the sea swept everything before it. Huge baskets filled with gravel for ballast plummeted down the passageway between the ponies, breaking up stalls as they went by.

Suddenly the galleon shuddered. From bow to stern came an endless rasping sound! The ship had struck a shoal. And with a ripping and crashing of timber the hull cracked open. In that split second the captain, his men, and his live cargo were washed into the boiling foam.

The wildcat sea yawned. She swallowed the men. Only the captain and fifteen ponies managed to come up again. The captain bobbed alongside the stallion and made a wild grasp for his tail, but a great wave swept him out of reach.

The stallion neighed encouragement to his mares, who

were struggling to keep afloat, fighting the wreckage and the sea. For long minutes they thrashed about helplessly, and just when their strength was nearly spent, the storm died as suddenly as it had risen. The wind calmed.

The sea was no longer a wildcat. She became a kitten, fawning and lapping about the ponies' legs. Now their hooves touched land. They were able to stand! They were scrambling up the beach, up on Assateague Beach, that long, sandy island which shelters the tidewater country of Virginia and Maryland. They were far from the mines of Peru.

Pony in the Dark
K. M. Peyton

Storm, a Shetland pony, born to the sound of gulls and used to breathing the fresh air of the Shetland Isles, is sold to become a pit pony.

STORM didn't like being shut in a stable and tied up all the time. The food they gave him was dry and strange. He had always found his own food before. But now there was no choice, just this bucket of funny stuff. But it tasted quite nice. He got used to it. He got used to all the strange harness they hung on him. And learnt how to pull a wagon. They put him side by side with an old pony at first, and he had to go with him whether he liked it or not.

When he had learnt to pull, he went by himself, first with an empty wagon, then with a load. They put a collar round his neck, and he learnt to pull into it. Sometimes he had to pull very hard to make it move at all. But he got pats and titbits when he did it right. If he got cross and kicked out, he was hit with a stick. This was painful and gave him a great surprise.

He was not alone. Six ponies were being broken in. Some of them kicked far more than Storm, and one was sent back to the dealer for being too naughty.

"But this is a good'un," the horsemaster said. "He'll do well."

The day came when Storm was ready to go down the mine. He did not know what was in store for him. He took daylight and fresh air and the sky for granted and did not know that he wasn't going to see them again for a very long time. He was taken to the pit-head where the cage came up out of the ground. He was used to this place now, with its din, the crashing and grinding of machinery. Usually he just stood there, getting used to it, but this time he was pushed roughly into the cage after the men streamed out, and the gate clanged behind him. Then the ground dropped beneath his hooves and he was whirling down through the darkness. He was terrified! All his senses left him and he shook so hard his legs nearly gave way. Whatever was happening?

But then his insides gave a great lurch and everything was still again. The metal gate clanged open, and he saw dimly-lit tunnels going in both directions ahead of him. A boy stood there.

"Come on, littl'un."

The voice was gentle. But Storm could not move for fear. The smell and the heat were foreign to him and he had to stand to take it all in, trying to allay his fear. The boy was patient and kind. But then he pulled on his bridle and said, "Come on, we can't stand here all day." But where had the day gone?

So Storm let himself be led. The sweat gathered on his thick coat in the strange hot air. Wherever was he? He went on in the hope that somewhere ahead he would come to a field of grass and a view of the sky.

But all he came to, after a long walk, was an underground stable, a long row of stalls with lamps hanging from the ceiling to make a dim light. The stalls were occupied by ponies whose presence reassured him. They seemed unafraid and were eating happily from their mangers. The walls were whitewashed and the place was clean and the air fresher. The boy led him into an empty stall and tied him up. A feed was waiting in the manger. Storm plunged his nose into it. This was something he recognized, at least.

Maybe the worst was over.

And so Storm's life as a pit pony began. He was put in the care of a boy called Barney, whose job was to harness Storm up to take empty tubs along the tunnels to the coal-hewers. The tub wheels ran on metal tracks, like a train. The hewers threw the coal into the tubs and Storm pulled the full tubs back to the pit-shaft. From there the coal was

taken by machinery up to the ground, and Storm went back again with the empty tubs.

The work never stopped, both men and ponies working in shifts day and night. Not that day or night meant anything underground. Storm forgot that there was such a thing as daytime. He just knew feed time and rest time and work time. The work was hard, the coal tubs very heavy, and the tunnels only just big enough for the pony and tub to get through. Sometimes the roof scraped on Storm's back. Sometimes rocks fell down and blocked the rails and Barney had to heave them out of the way. Apart from Barney's feeble lamp there was no light at all, and sometimes when the lamp failed, Storm had to find his way in total darkness, with Barney trusting himself to the pony's instinct.

It was very hot and Storm's heavy mane and tail were cut off and his coat clipped to make him more comfortable. Barney laughed at him and called him, "My little Ratty, my little scraped Ratty!" His proper name, Storm, was written on a board over his manger, but Barney often called him Ratty. Barney brought him titbits and sometimes a bag of grass. Storm had almost forgotten what grass tasted like. When Barney stopped for his "bait" – his little parcel of lunch and bottle of cold tea – he would share an apple with Storm and give him all his crusts of bread.

Barney had worked in the mine ever since he left school at fourteen. His father was a miner and worked hewing the coal. He crouched down under the low roof hacking away at the coal with a pickaxe and throwing it into the tub. Barney would be a coal-hewer when he was older and stronger. It was very hard work. The men just wore shorts because it was so hot and they sweated so, and the coal-dust stuck to their sweat so that they were black all over when they finished work. Their eyes gleamed in their black faces, but they laughed and joked, and only swore when the empty tubs didn't get back in time, or the timbers that held the roof up started to creak.

Sometimes the roof fell in. Sometimes men were buried alive, and sometimes ponies too. Storm was very aware of the messages the creaking pit-poles sent as they supported the roof, and sometimes he stopped, too scared to go on when he thought it wasn't safe. Then Barney would get frightened too, and wait with him in the sweating dark until the creaking stopped, or there was a rockfall ahead and more work to do to clear it.

Storm learnt what he had to do, and would get into the right position without Barney telling him, push the ventilation doors open with his nose, back up against the tubs when they pushed on him running down the hill.

"You're a clever one," Barney told him.

Storm never kicked or bit or got stubborn.

"One of the best," said the ostler who ran the stables. So if a pony was off sick Storm would stand in for him because he was no trouble, and work a double shift. Sometimes he worked for twenty-four hours without stopping.

But he was strong and well fed. He forgot about the sky

and the fields and the smell of the Atlantic ice wind and the cries of the gulls. In his dark stinking hole he did all that was asked of him. One of the best.

Unicorn
Peter Dickinson

In the dark forest, Rhiannon meets a fabulous silvery-white animal, very like a horse, with a single spiral horn growing from its forehead.

RHIANNON was an orphan and lived with her grandmother in a village at the edge of the forest. She was one of Sir Brangwyn's orphans, as they called them in those parts – that is to say her parents were alive but her father was imprisoned in the dungeons of Castle Grim and her mother worked in the castle kitchens to earn money to pay for his food. He had done nothing wrong, but Sir Brangwyn had accused him of stealing deer. Sir Brangwyn liked to have the best men from all the villages in his dungeons, so that the other villagers would stay quiet and good, and hardly dare murmur when he taxed them of every farthing they had. Everyone knew that Rhiannon's father was innocent. If he had really been stealing deer, Sir Brangwyn would have hanged him from the nearest tree.

Rhiannon was not allowed to go with her parents to the castle. Sir Brangwyn made a point of leaving the children behind, to remind the other villagers to be good. So she stayed in the village and did her share of the work. Everybody in the village had to work or starve, and since Rhiannon was only nine her job was to hunt in the forest for truffles.

The forest was enormous – nobody knew how big, or what lay deep inside it. Some said that strange beasts laired there, dragons and unicorns and basilisks, which could turn you to stone by looking at you. Others said all that had happened in the old days, and the strange beasts were gone, so now there were only ordinary animals such as boars and deer and wolves and bears. Sometimes Sir Brangwyn would come and hunt these. Hunting was the one thing he cared about in all the world.

Rhiannon never went deep into the forest. She always stayed where she could see the edge. Truffles are hard to find. They are a leathery black fungus which grows underground on the roots of certain trees, and for those who like rich food (as Sir Brangwyn did) they add a particularly delicious taste and smell. Rhiannon always hoped that one day she would find so many truffles that Sir Brangwyn would send her parents home as a reward, but it did not happen. She seldom found more than a few, and sometimes she would dig in forty places and find none.

Exactly a year after the soldiers had come to take her father away, Rhiannon went off to the forest as usual. But, not at all as usual, she was followed back that evening by a small white horse no more than a foal, pure silvery white with a silky mane and tail.

The villagers were amazed.

"It must have escaped from some lord's stable," they said, and they tried to catch it, thinking there would be a reward. But before they came anywhere near, away it darted, glimmering across the meadows and into the dark woods. Then they found, to their further amazement, that Rhiannon's basket was full of truffles.

"My little horse showed me where to dig," she said.

This seemed very good news. Sir Brangwyn's tax-clerk would be coming to the village in a few days' time. Truffles were rare and expensive. Perhaps they could pay all their taxes in truffles, and that would mean they would have a little food to spare for themselves this year. So next morning a dozen men and women went up with Rhiannon to the forest, hoping the little horse would come and show them where to dig. But they saw no sign of it and they found nothing for themselves, so at noon they went back to their own tasks, leaving Rhiannon behind. Again that evening the white horse came glimmering behind her almost to the edge of the village, then dashed away. And again Rhiannon's basket was full of truffles.

So it went on every day until the tax-clerk came, and the headman brought him a whole sackload of truffles to pay the taxes. This clerk was a monk, who could read and write. He knew things which ordinary people did not know. When he asked how it happened that the village had so many truffles to send, the headman told him. The headman was a simple fellow. (Sir Brangwyn saw to it that the clever ones were in his dungeons.)

That evening, the clerk sent for a huntsman and told him what he wanted, and next night the huntsman came back and told what he had seen. He had followed Rhiannon up to the forest, taking care to keep out of sight, and at the forest edge a little white horse had come cavorting out and kissed Rhiannon on the forehead, and then she had followed it in under the trees where it had run to and fro, sniffling and snuffling like a dog, and every now and then it would stop and paw with its hoof on the ground, and Rhiannon would dig there and find truffles. The horse was obviously extremely shy of anyone but Rhiannon and kept looking nervously around, so the huntsman had not been able to come close, but then, when Rhiannon's basket was full, she had sat down with her back against a tree and the horse had knelt by her side and put its head in her lap and gazed into her eyes and she had sung to it. The little horse had been so entranced that it seemed to forget all danger, and the huntsman had been able to creep close enough to see it well.

"And sure, it's a very fine wee beast, your honour," he

said to the clerk. "What it'll be doing in these woods I can't be guessing. And it's never seen bit or bridle, I'll be bound, never seen stall nor stable. As for the colour of its coat, it is whiter than snow, not a touch nor fleck of grey nor of yellow in it. Only one thing…"

"Yes?" whispered the clerk, as though he knew what was coming.

"The pity of it is the animal's face, for it's misshapen. It has this lump, or growth, as it might be, big as my bent thumb between the eyes."

"Ah," said the clerk.

Next morning he left his tax-gathering and hurried to Castle Grim to tell Sir Brangwyn there was a unicorn in the woods.

The great hall of Castle Grim was hung with the trophies of Sir Brangwyn's hunting. Deer and hare, boar and badger, wolf and fox, heron and dove, he had ridden it down or dug it up or hawked it out of the air. But he had never hunted unicorn. Before the clerk had finished his message Sir Brangwyn was on his feet and bellowing for his huntsmen and his grooms, and in an hour he was on the road with a dozen expert trackers and twenty couple of hounds.

The people of Rhiannon's village were glad to see him come. Sometimes when a village had shown him good sport he had let the people off their taxes for a whole year. So here they were eager to help. They beat the woods, they dug traps where they were told, they set watch, but it was all no use. Sir Brangwyn's clever hounds bayed to and fro and found nothing. His trackers found the prints of an unshod foal all over the truffle-grounds, but lost the trail among the trees.

After three days of this, Sir Brangwyn's temper soured, and the villagers began to be anxious. Then the tax-clerk explained what Sir Brangwyn had been too impatient to hear before, that the only way to hunt a unicorn is to send a maiden alone into the woods, and the unicorn will come to her and lay its head in her lap and be so enraptured by her singing that he will not see the huntsmen coming.

Sir Brangwyn had not brought any maidens with him, but the village headman told him about Rhiannon. All that night the villagers toiled by torchlight, cutting brushwood and building a great bank of it by the truffle-grounds, high enough to hide a mounted man. In the morning they took Rhiannon up to the forest. When they told her what she had to do she tried to say no, but by this time Sir Brangwyn had learnt where her parents were, and he explained to her what would happen to them if she refused. So she went into the forest and sat down, weeping, in her usual place, while Sir Brangwyn waited hidden behind the bank of brushwood.

For a long while everything was still.

Then, suddenly, there was a glimmering deep in the dark wood and the unicorn came delicately out, looking this way and that, hesitating, sniffing the wind. When it was sure all was safe it cavorted up to Rhiannon and kissed her on the forehead and knelt by her side with its head on her lap, gazing up into her eyes, puzzled why she did not sing. Sir Brangwyn broke from his hide, spurring the sides of his horse till the blood runnelled. The nearing hooves drubbed like thunder.

Then Rhiannon could bear it no more. She jumped to her feet with her arms round the unicorn's neck, dragging it up, and turned its head so that it could see Sir Brangwyn coming.

At once it reared away, giving Rhiannon no time to loose her hold. The movement twitched her sideways and up so that she was lying along the unicorn's back with her arms round its neck and the unicorn was darting away under the trees with Sir Brangwyn hallooing behind, his spear poised for the kill.

The hoof beats dwindled into the forest, into silence. Then huntsmen and villagers, waiting out of sight beyond the forest, heard a voice like the snarl of trumpets, a man's shout and a crash. Then silence once more.

The trackers followed the hoofprints deep into the dark wood. They found Sir Brangwyn's body under an oak tree, pierced through from side to side. His horse they caught wandering close by.

Rhiannon came out of the forest at sunset. What had she seen and heard? What fiery eye, what silvery mane? What challenge and what charge? She would not say.

Only when her mother and father came home, set free

by Sir Brangwyn's heir, she told them something. They had taken her to her bed and were standing looking down at her, full of their happiness in being all three together again, and home, when she whispered four words.

"Unicorns have parents too."

Horses to the Rescue

I know what it's like to be rescued by a pony! Once my
family and I enjoyed a wonderful horse-drawn caravan
holiday in Ireland. The caravan was drawn by Tom, a giant
shire horse, and we also hired a riding pony, Blanco.
All went well until we set off across a sandy bay to an
island. We had been assured it was perfectly safe as long as
we kept moving. But halfway across, Tom stopped and
the caravan's wheels sank into the soft sand. No matter
how we tried we could not get the caravan to move.
And the tide was coming in.
Blanco came to our rescue. She carried me at breakneck
speed across soft sand, boggy peat fields and clear round
the island before we met some tourists, who helped,
with their added weight, to get the caravan moving.

In the Russian folk-tale "Chestnut Grey", Ivan makes
friends with a magical horse who comes to his aid when he
seeks the hand in marriage of the fair Princess Elena.

In the final story, a young knight who is in love with the daughter of a rich duke is turned away because he is so poor. Fortunately, he owns the most beautiful horse in the land — "The Grey Palfrey" — who comes to the rescue!

Chestnut Grey

retold by Helen Cooper

*"Chestnut Grey, hear and obey!" With these words
Ivan summons a magical horse. But will they be able to leap
as high as the tip-top window of a very tall tower?*

A MAN once bought himself a farm and moved in with his three sons, well pleased with his beautiful new barley field. But he wasn't pleased very long. On Midsummer's Eve something came, and gobbled, and trampled the barley field flat.

Well, this happened once, and it happened twice, and the poor farmer didn't know what to do.

"*I'll* catch the thief," said the eldest son. "I'll watch the field all night from the barn." And the second son agreed to go too.

Ivan the youngest son thought his own thoughts and said nothing for no one ever listened to him.

It was warm and drowsy in the barn when the two eldest sons crept in that night. They had promised not even to close their eyes, but the straw was so soft that soon they slept.

The next day the field looked a terrible mess.

"But we didn't sleep a wink!" they lied.

"Ivan shall watch the field tonight," said the poor farmer. "But he's so useless, he's bound to do even worse than you!"

Ivan said nothing, just thought his own thoughts. But that night he didn't go into the barn. He held a rope in one hand, a bread bun in the other, and sat in the gloom wide-eyed and munching.

Just as the clock struck midnight, a magical horse thundered into the field. So swiftly he galloped, sparks flew from his hooves. So swiftly, the sky seemed to reel and shake.

The horse began to eat, and he trampled even more than he ate. But Ivan stole up, threw a rope round his neck, and quick as a wink was astride his back. How that horse did buck and kick, how he reared and galloped, screamed and pranced!

But Ivan laughed and held on tight, and though they battled half the night, the horse couldn't throw him off.

At last the horse gave up the fight. "If only you'll let me go," he pleaded, "I'll come to your aid whenever you need me."

"First," insisted Ivan sternly, "give me your solemn

word that you'll never spoil our barley again."

The horse bowed his head and promised. "Remember this," he said. "If ever you need me, just clap your hands three times and say, *Chestnut Grey, hear and obey!* and I'll be there before you can blink."

When Ivan told of all he had done, his family fell about laughing.

"A talking horse?" they mocked. "What nonsense!"

Nonsense or not, the barley field was never trampled again, but Ivan got no thanks for that.

Far away in the city, strange news was astir. Princess Elena the Fair had declared she would only marry the horseman who could leap up to her high window and take the ring from her finger.

Nothing would change her mind. The king was in despair. So he sent out his heralds to announce a day when all the horsemen in the land might try to win the princess's hand.

The two older brothers thought themselves very fine horsemen, and they boasted their fortunes were made.

Ivan sat quietly and said nothing. Secretly he didn't think much of their bragging, and he was relieved when they left.

He strolled out to a quiet glade, clapped his hands three times and called, "Chestnut Grey, hear and obey!" Before his voice had died away, into the glade galloped Chestnut Grey. He circled once and came to a halt before Ivan.

"I thought you'd call," snorted Chestnut Grey, "and now

it's time to be on our way. For I can jump as high as a hayrick, as high as a house, as high as a forest." And he lashed the air with his swirling tail.

"But I can't meet the princess like this," complained Ivan, looking down at his torn clothes.

"No, you can't go in those," agreed Chestnut Grey, "but climb into my left ear and out through my right, and then we'll see."

"Climb into your ear?" gasped Ivan. "How can I?"

"Just try," said Chestnut Grey.

So Ivan tried. To his surprise, it was the easiest thing in the world, and he came out dressed like a prince.

"Now we're ready!" cried Chestnut Grey, and they galloped away to the city.

In the centre of the city was a busy square, in the square was a tower, and right at the tip-top window of that tower sat Princess Elena the Fair. She looked beautiful enough to make your heart stop.

All the young men gathered there. They galloped and leapt, and leapt and galloped, until their fine horses were all in a lather – but not one could get near the princess.

Then Chestnut Grey raced into the square. He snorted and leapt up into the sky, higher than any of the other horses, high enough even to clear a house, but not high enough to reach the princess's window.

"Quick! Let's be off," whispered Ivan, and away they sped before anyone could stop them.

"That tower is a ridiculous height!" grumbled Ivan's

brothers when they came home that night. "Only one man got anywhere near, and after one leap even he disappeared."

"Maybe I should come tomorrow," said Ivan from his fireside chair.

"You wouldn't stand a chance," they scoffed. "And what princess would look at you?"

Ivan said nothing, just thought his own thoughts. But next day he summoned Chestnut Grey, climbed into the horse's left ear and out through the right, and came out even more splendidly dressed than the first time.

There was silence as they raced into the square. Chestnut Grey snorted, and leapt up into the sky. Higher than any of the other horses, high enough even to clear a forest, but still not quite high enough to reach the princess's window.

On the last day of the contest, Ivan summoned Chestnut Grey one more time. "Today you must jump as you've never jumped before!" he pleaded.

The horse nodded his great head, and lashed the air with his wild tail. Then they galloped into the city, and on into the square.

Chestnut Grey snorted, and leapt to the sky. Higher than any other horse, higher than ever he'd leapt before, high enough for Ivan to kiss the princess, and take the ring from her finger.

The crowd cheered and whistled and waved – they all wanted to greet the champion. But Ivan got away. They could not find him anywhere.

Three whole days went by, and the princess's future bridegroom was nowhere to be found. Ivan was hiding himself away with a rag wrapped around the ring on his finger. He tried not to think of the princess, for surely no princess would want to marry an ordinary farmer's son.

But once more the king sent his heralds out, to every part of the land. He commanded all his subjects to attend a grand banquet. No one dared disobey, and even Ivan had to be there.

All the guests were seated at oak tables laden with food. But Ivan withdrew to a shadowy corner, well away from the feasting.

Elena the Fair moved among the guests. She searched every table, she searched every face without success. Then, in the darkest corner of all, she found Ivan.

"Take that rag off your hand," she said with a smile.

Ivan unwound the rag, and there, to everyone's surprise, sparkled the princess's ring. The princess didn't mind his old torn clothes – she just led him up to the king. And the king welcomed Ivan into his family.

For the last time, Ivan summoned Chestnut Grey, and his old rags melted away and were transformed into wedding clothes.

Then Chestnut Grey proudly carried Ivan and his beautiful bride to the church.

The Grey Palfrey
retold by Barbara Leonie Pickard

*Set in France in the Middle Ages when knights were bold
and rode fine horses, this folk-tale tells how the grey palfrey
proves to be a young knight's greatest friend.*

IN the county of Champagne there once lived a knight.
He was young and handsome and brave, and indeed
he was all things that a good knight should be; but he
was poor, owning little land and only one small manor set
in a forest, among the trees and away from the road.

This young knight went much to the tourneying, often
going many miles from his home to where tournaments
were being held, not only for the sake of the honour he
would gain by his courage and skill, but for the prizes and
for the ransoms he might ask from those he overthrew, for
it was by these ransoms that he lived and bought all that
was needed for himself and for his servants and his few

followers. Though his garments were always neat and his helmet and his hauberk polished bright, his clothes were plain and his armour none of the best, and the food he ate, though there was enough of it, was no rich fare.

But one thing this knight owned that would not have shamed the wealthiest lord, and that was a grey palfrey, the favourite among his few horses, with sleek and glossy hide and a mane and a tail like flowing silver, so that no one, seeing it, did not stop to admire. Very fleet was this palfrey, and it had not its match in all Champagne. It was the envy of the countryside, and many were the rich lords who sought to buy it from the knight. Yet poor as he was, not for all the wealth in the world would he have parted with his palfrey, for he counted it his friend; and so indeed it proved to be.

Some two miles from this knight's manor, beside the road which ran through the forest, stood the castle of a duke. Old he was, and rich, and very miserly, forever seeking to add wealth to wealth. He had one daughter, the only young and gracious thing in all his castle, and it was this maiden whom the poor knight loved, and she loved him in return. But because he was poor, though of good repute, her father would never have considered him as a suitor; and since the maiden was never permitted to leave the castle, they might only speak together secretly, through a crack in the castle wall.

Every day at the same hour, when he was not at the tourneying, the knight would ride on the grey palfrey from his manor to the castle of the duke, by a secret path through the forest which he alone used. And every day when she might, the maiden would await his coming at the castle wall, and they would talk of their love for a few happy moments. But not every day could she leave her father's side, or steal away unobserved, so on many days the knight would wait in vain to see her before riding sadly home along the secret path. Yet this made the times when they met all the sweeter.

One day the knight could bear it no longer, and since he knew the maiden cared nothing for riches, and would have been content as his wife had he been a peasant and lived in a hovel, he went to the castle and asked to speak with her father. The old duke welcomed him courteously, since fair words cost nothing, and the young knight said, "Lord, there is a favour I would ask of you."

"And what might it be?" said the duke.

"I am poor," said the knight, "but I am nobly born, and my honour is unquestioned, and no man has ever been able to speak ill of me. I love your daughter and I know that she loves me. I am here to ask for her hand in marriage."

The old duke went as pale as his white beard in his anger. "There is not a lord in all France, nor a prince in all Christendom, whom I could not buy for my daughter, if I wished her to marry. She is not for a poor knight such as you. Now begone from my castle and never speak to me of such matters again."

Heavy at heart, the knight rode home, but since the

maiden loved him he did not lose all hope, and a day or two later he rode to a distant town where a great tournament was to be held, thinking that there he might win a small measure of those riches which, if carefully saved, might cause the old duke to relent.

At that time a lord, wealthy and old as the duke himself, came to visit him, and after they had talked long together of the things they had done when young and the memories they had in common, the lord said, "We are both rich, but were our riches combined, they would be even greater. Were you to give me your daughter as a wife, I would ask no dowry with her, but you and I, thus linked by a marriage, might share our wealth for the rest of our days. What say you to this, my old friend?"

The duke was glad and rubbed his hands together and nodded many times. "You have spoken well, it shall be as you say. In all France there will be none richer than we two."

The duke set about preparations for the marriage and cared nothing for his daughter's tears, inviting some score or more guests for the wedding, old friends of his and the bridegroom's, greybeards all. And because of his avarice, he sent to his neighbours in the countryside, asking the loan of a horse or two from each, that there might be mounts enough to carry the guests and their squires along the road through the forest to the church. And so little shame he had, that he sent to the young knight to borrow his grey palfrey, that his daughter might ride to her wedding on the finest horse in all Champagne.

The young knight had returned from the tourneying, well pleased enough with life, for he had easily been the best of all the knights gathered there, and every prize he had carried home to his little manor in the forest; so that it seemed to him he was perhaps a step nearer that which he had set his heart upon. When he heard the duke's message, he asked, "Why does your master wish to borrow my horse?"

And the duke's servant answered, "So that my master's daughter may ride upon it tomorrow to her wedding at the church."

When the young knight learnt how the maiden he loved was to marry the old lord, he thought that his heart would break, and at first he would have refused with indignation the duke's request. But then he thought, "Not for the sake of her father, but to do honour to the lady I love, will I lend my palfrey. It is I whom she loves, she will have no joy of this marriage, and perhaps it will comfort her a little if I send her the palfrey which is my friend." So he saddled and bridled the palfrey and gave it to the serving-man, and then he went to his own room and would neither eat nor drink, but flung himself down upon his bed and wept.

In the duke's castle, on the eve of the wedding, his guests made merry, feasting and drinking deep, and since they were, like himself, all old, when the time came for them to go to rest, they were in truth most weary. But very early in the morning, before dawn indeed, while the moon still shone brightly, the watchman roused them that they might be at the church betimes. Grumbling and half asleep, the guests clothed themselves and gathered in the courtyard where their horses waited. Yawning, they climbed into the saddles and set out upon their way, with the duke and the old lord at their head. And after all the others came the maiden on the grey palfrey, with her father's old seneschal to watch over her. She was clad in a fair gown, and over it a scarlet mantle trimmed with costly fur, but her face was pale and she wept, and she had not slept all night for sorrow.

In the moonlight they left the castle and took the forest road which led to the church; yet since the way was narrow and branches overhung the track, they might not ride two abreast, but followed each other one by one through the forest, with the old seneschal at the very end, after the weeping bride.

A little way along the road, from habit, the palfrey turned aside, taking the secret path that its master had so often used; and because the old seneschal was nodding and dozing as he rode, he never missed the maiden. Deep into the forest, along the secret way went the palfrey, and in terror the maiden looked about her. But though she was fearful, she did not cry out, for she thought, I had rather be lost in the forest and devoured by the wild beasts, than live without the knight I love. And she let the palfrey carry her where it would.

After two miles, in the dim light of early dawn, the

palfrey stopped before a small manor set among the trees and waited for the gate to be opened. The watchman peeped out through a grille and called, "Who is there?" And, trembling, the maiden answered, "I am alone and lost in the forest. Have pity on me and give me shelter till sunrise."

But the watchman, looking closely, knew his master's palfrey, and made all haste to where he was. "Lord," he said, "at the gate stands your palfrey, and on its back is a lady so lovely that I think she can be no mortal maid. Is it your will that I should let her in?"

The young knight leapt off his bed and ran to the gate and flung it wide and caught the maiden in his arms. When they had done with kissing and weeping for joy, he asked her, "How did you come here?"

And she answered, "It was your grey palfrey that brought me, for I should not have known the way."

"Since you are here," said the knight, "here shall you stay, if you will it."

"It is all I ask, to be with you for ever," she said.

So the knight called for his chaplain, and with no delay he and the maiden were married, and in all the manor there was great rejoicing.

When the duke and the old lord and their friends reached the church they found that the maiden was not with them, and they set themselves to search for her, all about the forest. But by the time the duke came upon the little manor set among the trees, his daughter was a wife, and there was nothing he could do about it, save give the marriage his blessing, which he did with an ill grace. But little the young knight and his lady cared for that.

Acknowledgements

The editor and publisher gratefully acknowledge permission
to reprint the following:

Extract from *The Orange Pony* © Wendy Douthwaite
Reprinted by permission of Macmillan Children's Books, London, UK

"The Battle" from *The Snow Pony* by Alison Lester
First published in Sydney in 2001
Reprinted by permission of Allen & Unwin Book Publishers, Australia

The Mud Pony, retold by Caron Lee Cohen
© 1988 Caron Lee Cohen
Reprinted by permission of Scholastic Inc.

The Gift Horse © 2005 June Crebbin

Extract from *War Horse* text © 1987 Michael Morpurgo
Used with permission of Egmont Books Ltd

Extract from *I Rode a Horse of Milk White Jade* by Diane Lee Wilson
© 1997 Diane Lee Wilson
Reprinted by permission of Orchard Books, published by Scholastic Inc.

"Live Cargo!" reprinted with the permission of Simon & Schuster Books
for Young Readers, an imprint of Simon & Schuster Children's
Publishing Division, from *Misty of Chincoteague* by Marguerite Henry
© 1947 and renewed © 1975 Marguerite Henry

ACKNOWLEDGEMENTS

Extract from *Pony in the Dark* by K. M. Peyton, published by Corgi
Used by permission of Transworld Publishers,
a division of The Random House Group Ltd

"Unicorn" from *Merlin Dreams* by Peter Dickinson
Reprinted by permission of A. P. Watt Ltd on behalf of
The Hon. Peter Dickinson

From *Chestnut Grey* by Helen Cooper published by
Frances Lincoln Ltd, © Frances Lincoln 1993
Text © Helen Cooper 1993
Reproduced by permission of Frances Lincoln Ltd, London, UK

"The Grey Palfrey" from *French Legends, Tales and Fairy Stories*
retold by Barbara Leonie Picard (OUP, 1992)
© Barbara Leonie Picard 1955
Reprinted by permission of Oxford University Press

First published 2005 by Walker Books Ltd
87 Vauxhall Walk, London SE11 5HJ

2 4 6 8 10 9 7 5 3 1

Introductions and this selection © 2005 June Crebbin
Illustrations © 2005 Inga Moore

The rights of the authors of the works comprising this anthology
and the rights of the illustrator have been asserted by them in
accordance with the Copyright, Designs and Patents Act 1988

This book has been typeset in Calligraphic and Centaur

Printed in China

British Library Cataloguing in Publication Data:
a catalogue record for this book is
available from the British Library

ISBN 0-7445-9278-X

www.walkerbooks.co.uk

For all my friends at
Somerby Equestrian Centre
J. C.

For Bertie
I. M.